"I aim to pl

"But to be honest, where you're concerned my thoughts aren't very gentlemanly," Cade continued, before leaning in and kissing Patience. He meant it to be a soft taste, but at first contact she pressed herself into him, and Cade's instincts took over. He gently twisted a hand in her hair so he could tilt her head to better explore her mouth.

"Cade," she whispered against his lips.

"Yes." His breathing was heavy. All he wanted to do was take her upstairs and make love to her until the morning. For a moment, her hand traveled down his hip and he thought she might cup him. The mere hint of her touch made him harden into a brick.

When Patience suddenly stepped away from him, he groaned.

"Didn't we promise your grandmother we'd be there by eight?"

He grunted and leaned his forehead against hers. "You don't play fair."

"Oh, I can think of all kinds of games we can play later. And none of them will be fair," she promised.

Dear Reader,

I used to spend a great many of my summers in East Texas where my grandparents had a farm. It was a way for my parents to get cheap summer babysitting, but I also learned useful skills like how to ride a horse, shell peas, oh, and the most important one, how to flirt with boys.

When I decided to write my first cowboy story, *Truth and Dare*, I looked back to those country summers. Skiing on the lake, dances where the whole town turned out and there were so many handsome cowboys. Cade, my hero, is an amalgamation of those guys, with a little bit of my husband thrown in. He's from good solid stock and he's a man who goes after what he wants.

And he wants Patience.

She isn't sure what to make of Cade. All she wants to do is solve her first case and get back to her nice safe lab. Cade is anything but safe, and the more she gets to know him, the tougher it is for her to keep up her emotional walls. Will she be able to step out of her shell to be with this incredible guy? The answer awaits you in *Truth and Dare.*

Please email me at candacehavensbook@gmail.com and tell me what you think about the book. You can also find me on Twitter.com/candacehavens and MySpace, Facebook and Live Journal, all of which you can find on www.candacehavens.com.

Enjoy!

Candace Havens

Candace Havens

TRUTH AND DARE

TORONTO NEW YORK LONDON
AMSTERDAM PARIS SYDNEY HAMBURG
STOCKHOLM ATHENS TOKYO MILAN MADRID
PRAGUE WARSAW BUDAPEST AUCKLAND

Recycling programs
for this product may
not exist in your area.

ISBN-13: 978-0-373-79617-5

TRUTH AND DARE

ABOUT THE AUTHOR

Award-winning author and columnist Candace "Candy" Havens lives in Texas with her mostly understanding husband, two children and two dogs, Scoobie and Gizmo. Candy is a nationally syndicated entertainment columnist for FYI Television. She has interviewed just about everyone in Hollywood from George Clooney and Orlando Bloom to Nicole Kidman and Kate Beckinsale. You can hear Candy weekly on The Big 96.3 in the Dallas–Fort Worth Area. Her popular online writer's workshop has more than thirteen hundred students and provides free classes to professional and aspiring writers.

Books by Candace Havens

HARLEQUIN BLAZE
523—TAKE ME IF YOU DARE
607—SHE WHO DARES, WINS

To my husband, Steve,
thank you for believing in my dreams

1

"YOUR FATHER IS DEAD."

It took a few seconds for the Phosphor County sheriff's cautious words to register. Cade Randall's chest tightened with pain, but he pushed the emotion away.

Figures the old man would show up today, of all days. Even dead he still caused trouble.

Cade didn't want to care about the man who abandoned his family twenty years ago. He glanced around the offices of Stonegate Investigative Agency wondering why the sheriff brought him here to tell him the news when a simple phone call would have sufficed.

The woman behind the desk watched him carefully. He struggled to remember her name—Patience something. He didn't know who she was, exactly. She was beautiful. A professor type, with long blond hair that framed a perfect face featuring high cheekbones and nearly translucent green eyes. She wore a suit jacket over a miniskirt, he recalled her legs were the kind men dreamed about. And she smelled like honeysuckle, which for some reason was the most distracting thing about her.

His father was dead.

Judging from the looks on the sheriff's face and Patience's, they were waiting for him to respond.

"Sheriff, I appreciate you letting me know."

He checked his phone. There were six messages from his executive assistant. "I'm sorry, but I need to go." The merger was happening today, and he couldn't be late for his next meeting. Cade rose to leave.

"Wait." Patience held out a hand as she stood. "Don't you want to know what happened to your father?" Her eyes narrowed with recrimination. To her, Cade probably looked like a heartless bastard.

"Ma'am, he left our family many years ago without so much as a goodbye. He just didn't come home one night. So, no, I don't care how he died, or where he was when you found him." He paused reflecting for a moment. There was someone who would care. "Though I'm certain my grandmother would like to give her son a proper burial."

"Please, hear me out." Her voice was firm. "I promise you I won't take more than two more minutes to explain."

Stubborn woman.

Cade didn't have time for any of this. He had to

get back to the office. Though something in her eyes compelled him to stand still. "Fine. You have my attention." He crossed his arms over his chest.

She didn't bother sitting down. "As the sheriff said, I'm Dr. Patience Clark, Stonegate's forensic anthropologist. Your father's remains were brought to Austin by the sheriff for identification."

Cade inclined his head slightly to let her know he understood.

"I'll cut to the chase, since you have no interest in what happened to him. I felt you should know your father was murdered about twenty years ago on some land just outside of your hometown."

Murdered?

In Phosphor?

The knot in Cade's chest tightened even more. That meant… No, she had to be wrong. Why was this happening now? His phone vibrated again and Cade took it out and glanced at it as the sheriff and Patience watched him.

His father didn't leave the family, after all. Cade rubbed his forehead and tried to process the information, but he couldn't. He couldn't deal with this today.

Cade shoved what Patience told him on a mental shelf. He'd deal with it after the merger. His employees were depending on him making this deal work.

"I apologize for my behavior and I appreciate you bringing this to my attention. Unfortunately, I have to go." He started to back out the door.

Patience gave him a wary glance. "One more minute, please." She pulled out a two-page document. "If you'll sign this, it'll give me permission to pursue your father's murder on your behalf, then I'll get out of your hair. You may not care who killed him, but my company, Stonegate Investigative Agency, has a one hundred percent close rate when consulting on cases. I need to find your father's murderer. The sheriff will be supervising the investigation."

Cade's gut burned with anxiety and he ran his fingers through his hair. He had to get out of there. "I'll sign anything you want, but I'm not sure what you think you're going to find after twenty years. Seems like a waste of time to me."

She pushed the documents toward him on the desk and pointed where she needed his signature. "My guess is you've never been on an archeological dig. You'd be surprised what can be found even after thousands of years. The sheriff told me the bones were discovered by hikers in a shallow grave that had been wasted away by erosion in a remote area, so if it's been untouched there's a good chance I'll find something."

"It's your time." He shoved the papers toward her.

"Thank you." She pulled the signed papers to her chest.

The lifted eyebrow told him she didn't approve of his attitude, but he couldn't worry about that. The merger about to take place meant big things for his company. The value of his employees' stocks would rise through the roof, and he could start the new research division for their microchip and have an entirely new brand of supercomputers out next year.

He shook the sheriff's hand and took Patience's hand in his. It was soft, and he had a feeling her scent would linger on his skin. "Thank you, again."

His phone buzzed, and he answered it.

"Sir, Greg is here and he says he has to talk to you now." His assistant was excited, which meant something had happened.

"Give me thirty seconds and then put him on."

Cade tried to smile at the sheriff and at Patience but was sure that it came off more as a grimace.

"Again, I appreciate your efforts." He turned to leave.

"Here," she said. "This is my information, in case you have any questions."

He stuffed the folded piece of paper into his pocket and hurried for the door, the phone at his ear.

As Greg spoke, he tried to listen, but his mind was on his father and the woman who had given him the news. While Cade usually didn't care what people believed of him, it bothered him that she might consider him a coldhearted jerk. Well, he could be when it came to business, but that was different.

"Cade, did you hear me? The meeting has been moved up to ten. You have to get here now," Greg yelled through the phone. Normally, Cade wouldn't take such insubordination from an employee, but Greg was also one of his best friends.

Cade slipped into the limo waiting for him and the driver shut the door.

"Greg, calm down. I'm on my way. I'll be there in five. We have plenty of time to go over any last-minute issues."

The other man went on to tell Cade some of the details, but he only half listened. He pulled the folded sheet from his jacket pocket. Her business card slipped out, the scent of honeysuckle filled his senses. He opened the piece of paper to find a brief note.

"I dare you to help me find your father's killer."

She'd met him less than ten minutes ago and she knew exactly how to get to him.

Cade wasn't sure how he felt about that.

PATIENCE SAT IN THE BASEMENT of Phosphor's County Courthouse, staring at six giant boxes of records. Her job usually involved identifying bones, some of which were centuries old. This was her first time to do any real detective work, something she normally left to others at the agency.

The seasoned professionals at Stonegate knew exactly how to tackle cold murder cases. With so many colleagues busy with other projects and a burning desire to get out of the lab, Patience couldn't let this case rest. She couldn't stand the idea of this poor man being murdered and no one caring enough to do something about it.

Her mind flashed to the sexy Cade Randall. The instant their eyes met, her body reacted with a heated blush. That sort of thing never happened to her and she'd been worried she might be coming down with a cold. But when those steely gray eyes of his had narrowed in on her, she could tell he was just as attracted to her as she was to him. Anthropologically speaking the reaction was an interesting phenomenon, one she wouldn't mind pursuing.

Too bad he's a jerk.

Shoving her hair up into a ponytail, she moved toward the boxes, grateful experienced agency detectives Shannon and Katie had given her advice on where to start. No one seemed to know who owned the land where the bones were discovered. Finding the answer was her first assignment on the well-ordered plan she'd devised.

"More than likely, no one wants to lay claim because they are worried about the consequences," Katie had informed her. "Some of the records may be really old, and property lines shift all the time. When land is inherited or sold and the surveyors don't know what they're doing, anything can happen. There have been cases where fifty years later a farmer discovers part of the land he's been working on most of his life, isn't his. Disputes over land, especially in Texas, are a big deal. It's a good place to start."

Lifting the lid on the first box, dust assaulted

Patience. She sneezed, and reached for a tissue in her bag. Evidently, people didn't hang out in the Phosphor records room very often. The whole place could use a vacuum and about a hundred dust rags. Patience had a slight case of OCD and preferred her spaces neat and tidy. She kept her labs pristine, and she wasn't a fan of moldy smelling dustbins like the basement.

Pulling out an armful of files she sat down at the long table and began to peruse them. For three hours she sat searching for one mention of the property in question. She didn't find a thing.

Her first day in town, and she was doing not so great. Frustrated, Patience returned everything to its proper place and put the lids back on the boxes.

Way to go, detective.

Her friends made it look so easy.

Glancing at her watch she realized it had been several hours since she'd eaten.

Guess it's time to check out the Bluebonnet Café.

She'd seen the establishment across the street when she parked in front of the courthouse. It was almost one and when she entered the café she could tell it had been a busy afternoon. Dishes were stacked high in a big tub behind the counter, and the waitresses were wiping down all the tables and refilling salt and pepper shakers.

"Hey, darlin', why don't you take that booth in the corner, we've got that one cleaned up for you," said the waitress with a long brunette ponytail, jeans and a pink T-shirt that read "Shut up and eat."

Patience nodded her thanks and walked toward the back. A group of older gentlemen sat at a center table. They looked like regulars, and she wondered if maybe she should try to talk to them to see if they knew who owned the property. But food was her first priority.

The menu was on the table, and from the delicious smells in the kitchen she had a feeling the selections were comfort food greatness. She ordered a cheeseburger, fries and lemonade. She thought seriously about a piece of coconut cake, before deciding the burger and fries would do enough damage.

She didn't mind her curves, unless they made her jeans too tight, which was why she usually stuck to meat, vegetables and fruit.

The waitress delivered her lunch, and Patience gasped. The hamburger was almost as big as the plate. Even with her appetite she would barely make a dent in the food.

A shadow crossed in front of her table. Patience glanced up to see three of the men from the other table standing over her.

"Hello." Patience was curious as to why they were there.

"Heard ya was over at the courthouse digging into property records," the oldest man said. He wore a dark gray hat, jeans and his skin was so leathery it didn't look real. His nearly black eyes were downright hostile, as was his tone.

"I might have been," Patience ventured. She didn't know what they were up to, but she refused to be intimidated. "I'm not sure how it concerns you, one way or the other." Her right eyebrow rose. She'd dealt with bullies all of her life, she could handle a couple of rednecks in a Podunk town.

"Quite a mouth you got there," said the youngest of the three, who was probably somewhere around fifty, though it was hard to tell with his black hat pulled down over his face so low she couldn't see his eyes. He leaned forward.

Patience refused to move, holding her chin even higher.

"Reckon you should keep to your own business and leave our town alone," the man threatened.

"I reckon you should leave my friend Patience there alone," said a voice from the doorway of the café. There was a silhouette of a man who wore a cowboy hat, white shirt, boots and jeans, but she couldn't see his face.

"Her business is my business," he continued, "and I don't appreciate you making threats to my friends."

The older man held his hands up in surrender.

"Just looking after the town, Cade. We don't like nosey folk in our business."

Cade walked to the table and Patience had to forcibly shut her mouth with her hand. The man had been sexy in his suit, but in these jeans, he was nothing less than smokin' hot, as her boss, Mariska, the owner of Stonegate, would say.

He leaned down and kissed her cheek. "Hey, there. Everything okay?"

His lips scorched her skin, and she couldn't breathe.

She nodded.

Cade slid into the other side of the booth. "I see you ordered enough for the both of us." He gave her a dazzling smile.

She willed her mouth to work, but it didn't. Though her heartbeat did double-time.

Cade glanced at the men. "Moses, Jim, Ralph, I'm sure you have better things to do than watch us eat." He smiled but his tone implied they should leave quickly.

Up until six weeks ago when he came to town to check on his land at his grandmother's request, it had been two years since Cade had been in Phosphor to visit his family. Not much had changed. For the most part the townspeople were friendly, but these old characters were the exception.

The men stared at him, but eventually backed away, mumbling as they left the café.

Cade jumped up to grab an empty plate from the waitress, and ordered a sweet tea.

Patience remembered the last time she'd seen him. He was like some kind of Jekyll and Hyde—a mind-bendingly sexy Jekyll and Hyde.

"Thanks," she said finally. "I could have handled them on my own."

Cade nodded. "I'm sure you could. But I don't like aggressive types, especially ones who pick on beautiful women."

He called her beautiful. No one had ever said that about her. The man was a flirt.

She cleared her throat. "What are you doing here?"

Cade took her fork and knife and cut the hamburger in half. Then he scooped a handful of fries and put everything on his plate.

"I'm taking your dare."

2

THE SUN SHINING THROUGH the diner windows danced along Patience's angelic locks giving the appearance of a halo, but Cade's thoughts weren't close to heavenly. The woman was more intoxicating than he had remembered and for the past week she'd been haunting his dreams.

Twice while closing the merger deal he'd lost track of what he'd been saying thanks to sudden visions of her face flashing in his mind. More than anything he wanted to wash away that look of disappointment she'd given him just before he'd walked out of her office.

He tried to convince himself that he'd been upset when they met and that he'd made her into much more than she was. But he was right the first time. He'd known that as soon as he walked into the café.

Taking a bite of his half of their hamburger, he studied her as she concentrated on her fries. She was obviously surprised to see him, and he'd arrived just in the nick of time. If she had any inkling of how he really felt, Patience would run straight back to Austin and lock her door.

If he had any brains at all, he'd do the same thing.

"Thanks for sharing your food with me."

A slow smile crept across her mouth. "Uh, sure. So, you came to help me out?"

"Thought it was the least I could do after being so rude to you the other day. I'm usually never rude to women." It was true. Many in the business community thought him to be cutthroat and they weren't wrong. Cade was driven and wanted to provide a solid company for his employees, most of them had been with him from the beginning and sometimes that meant making tough decisions. Combining his company's resources with that of another would in the long run make both companies stronger.

Patience pushed the stray hairs that had fallen from her ponytail behind her ears. "That's sexist in a way, you know."

He nodded. "You can blame my mom, and after she died, my grandmother. Gentlemen are always supposed to speak kindly to the ladies." He gave her his best sweet Southern accent. "I can honestly say I was in shock. All these years I thought my dad was some sorry bastard who ran off with another woman. Then I find out he'd been murdered." Cade took a sip of his tea.

"The sheriff explained as much, so I didn't hold it against you—much."

Cade had to stop himself from leaning across the table and kissing her when she smiled at him like that.

Whoa, boy, slow it down.

"So what were you doing that got those boys' attention?"

She shrugged. "I was going through old property records in the courthouse. I didn't find anything. If Moses had given me the chance, I would have told him he had nothing to worry about. And, well, there's something I need to tell you. I'm not sure you're going to like it, but I hope you'll give me a chance to explain."

Now he was curious. "I can't imagine anything you could say that would upset me, Patience." He liked the way her name sounded on his lips.

After glancing around the restaurant she leaned forward and put her elbows on the table. "I told you when we first met I'm a forensic anthropologist."

Cade had done some checking into her background before making the drive down to Phosphor. He'd discovered she was the best at what she did. She'd written several books, and universities around the world courted her and through the Stonegate Agency she consulted for law enforcement officials all over the world. She was the superstar of the forensic anthropology field.

"Normally, in a case like your father's, I identify

the remains and then one of the detectives from our agency would take over the case to track down the murderer."

Cade had a feeling he knew where this was going. "You're worried you don't have the right skill set to solve this."

"Yes and no." She twirled a fry. "I've been with the Stonegate Agency for some time now, and I've picked up a great deal from my friends. But I've never followed through on a case completely on my own."

"So why not assign the case to someone else?"

Patience shook her head. "There is no one else right now. We're short staffed in Austin as it is while some of our associates are away working around the world. It would be weeks, possibly months before one of the detectives could take on anything new. I felt like your father was long overdue for some peace, and I wanted to give that to him. And to your family."

Every time he thought of the word *murder* he had to pause to consider what it really meant. He had a lot of apologizing to do to the heavens for the many horrendous things he'd said through the years about his dad.

"As far as I'm concerned we couldn't have anyone better than you helping our family."

Patience sucked in a breath of surprise, her cheeks becoming a light shade of pink. "Why do you say that?"

"You're passionate about this or you wouldn't have taken time away from your lab and other cases." He

wanted to ask her why this was so important to her,
but something told him this wasn't the right time.
It was more a hunch than anything, but he also saw
sadness in her eyes. "You mentioned at your office
that the sheriff would be overseeing the investigation,
so I'm not totally understanding the problem."

She grinned.

Cade shifted in his seat like a nervous schoolboy
with a crush.

"I promise you I will do everything I can to find
who did this. They have to pay for what they did to
your family."

Cade was grateful someone cared enough to even
try. It couldn't be easy solving a twenty-year-old murder. "Well, I'll be here to help you, so we can cover
twice the ground at the same time. I do have to run
out to the ranch every once in a while to see how
things are going."

"The ranch?"

"Yeah, a couple of months ago I hired a foreman
to run my family's old place. We bought some cattle
and he's got the barn on the east side up and running.
I promised to help him with the fences while I was
here, and fixing up the old barn near the house. But
my dad comes first. That is if you want me."

WANT HIM? PATIENCE WANTED to tie him up in a
bow like a present and feast on him for weeks. She
couldn't remember the last time her libido had been
this fully engaged. He wasn't her normal brand of

"man candy," as her friends liked to say, but then what was normal? She hadn't been on an official date in years.

Technically he was a client and she had to be-have.

Katie broke the rule and she survived quite nicely.

Katie, one of Stonegate's best detectives, lived in London with her hot professor boyfriend. They'd met when Katie was protecting him. So maybe the rule wasn't so hard and fast after all.

The last thing Patience needed was romantic complications. It would take all her concentration and resources to find the murderer. Her gut told her it would be best to stay away from the handsome cowboy.

"I don't want you to take time away from the ranch, it sounds like it's important to you." She popped an-other French fry in her mouth. She'd have to run two or three miles to keep half of her lunch from landing on her hips.

"Oh, it's no problem. I'd planned on spending as much time as I can with you."

Patience's head snapped up. Did he say he wanted to spend time with her? From the moment they'd met in her office she'd experienced an inexplicable pull toward him. Had he felt the same?

"Helping with the case that is," he finished.

Her hopes sank. "Of course." She waved a hand to the waitress for the check.

"Ah, honey it's on the house," the waitress told her. "You got our Cade back to town, so I feel like we owe ya one." She leaned down and kissed Cade's cheek, wrapping her arms around his neck.

Something strange came over Patience and it took a second for her to realize her clenched fist might be a sign of jealousy. It wasn't an emotion she knew. There had never been anyone in her life to feel jealous about.

Interesting.

The scientist part of her brain wanted to explore the implications, but the woman in her was freaked out by her response.

Cade stood and gave the waitress a big bear hug.

Patience's stomach twisted into one huge knot.

"Charli, you are the best cousin ever, but I told you that's no way to run a business." He plopped a twenty down on the table. "You can't be giving the goods away for free."

"That ain't what you told all those girls in high school." She let out a loud laugh, but she didn't give him the money back.

Cousin? They were family.

"You keep this one," she said, pointing to Cade, "on the straight and narrow. Don't get his temper up or he's ornery as a hornet's nest on the first day of spring."

He made a ring motion above the top of his head indicating a halo. "Don't listen to her. I'm a complete angel." He fluttered his eyelashes angelically. "She's the one with the temper. Just ask her brother Jason. He woke up bald one morning because he said her boyfriend looked like a bean pole."

Charli slapped him on the hip with the rag. "Now don't you be tellin' tales." The other woman smiled at Patience. "But trust me that boy deserved it."

They all laughed. This man was the exact opposite of the one she had met at her office. She couldn't believe she thought him so cold and calculated. He was down-to-earth and relaxed. And she could see he had a great respect for his family.

Over at the courthouse, everyone seemed to have kind words for Cade. There were many cheerful hellos and pats on the back welcoming him to town. When she'd entered the first time she'd been completely ignored, except for the occasional curious glance.

"They're so much more friendly toward you," she said as they walked down the long staircase to the basement.

"What do you mean?" He helped her push open the large wooden door protecting the old records.

"When I first arrived, some of them looked at me like I was an exhibit at the zoo."

"Ah, well, they'll warm up to you soon enough. Everyone around here is cautious of strangers," he said as he held the door open for her.

"Like those men at the diner?"

He shrugged. "I'm not sure what's going on with them. I'll have a talk with them later."

There was no sense making more trouble. "Don't bother. That was probably their way of protecting their town from an outside threat. Though why they see me that way makes no sense."

"With those three there's absolutely no tellin'." Cade waved a hand in front of his face as they reached the dusty records room. "I'm guessing the spotless housekeeping upstairs doesn't make its way down here very often."

"From the looks of it, they pretty much use this as a storage room. Evidently no one in Phosphor ever has to do any research, because I found at least three inches of dust on most of the boxes. I wonder if they understand how much of their history is down here."

"What do you mean?" Cade took a deep breath and blew the dust from the top of a box they'd moved to the table.

"From an anthropological point of view, when people migrate to an area and when they leave can be based on a variety of factors. You can find information about certain eras where the town may have been booming because of river travel, or the railroads. From some of the mortgages and contracts I saw earlier, there seems to be an influx of ranchers buying up land around here over the last five years.

"Possibly they've had some good years without drought and the pastures are greener than normal. I don't know that for a fact, but it's something that can be found out with a little study. I find it fascinating."

She coughed from the dust. "I only wish other people found it as interesting as I do."

"Huh. I never thought about it that way. My cousins and I have all bought up land, or have come back to town to rebuild our family ranches that have gone to pasture."

"My first question would be why in the last five years?"

"I don't know about my cousins, but for me I finally had the income to do with the place what I always wanted. My plan is to have at least three hundred heads of longhorns in the next twenty-four months. I'd also like to fix up the old family house and make it a weekend and summerhouse. Somewhere I can get away from Austin and my life there."

"Makes sense. Do you feel a need to reconnect with your past and possibly spend time with your family? I find that is the motivation for most people when they return to their old homes."

Cade was scrutinizing her. "I guess so. I've been so caught up with my business I realized I hadn't spent Christmas with my grandmother in five years. She put her foot down when I forgot her birthday in February, and I guess that's when I started thinking about the ranch."

Patience knew there was more to his story, but she wasn't sure he was ready to examine that yet.

"Well, I guess we better get started opening these boxes. They aren't going to research themselves." He grinned at her.

"What I wouldn't give for a modern-day court-house with computer records." She smiled back at him. "But I guess this is why my friends call it grunt work."

Cade searched through twenty-year-old property deeds. Patience took on the task of reading through the more recent files. They hoped to meet in the middle somewhere.

"Hmm." She heard him murmur.

"Did you find something?" She peeked over the edge of the box she was going through.

"It's not so much about what is here, as what isn't. There are six months' worth of files missing."

Patience stood. "Maybe no one filed deeds during that time," she offered.

"No, it wouldn't matter. There were years when nothing was filed, but there were still file folders for those months. But it's the dates that really have me wondering."

"Why is that?"

"The missing files are the ones six months before my dad died."

3

"I SHOULD CALL THE SHERIFF with this information."
Patience drew the box toward her and replaced the
documents. "For all we know, he may have the files
in his office. He said he'd do some preliminary work
before I arrived."

She slammed a box lid down. "I didn't even let
him know I was in town. I probably could have saved
myself a lot of trouble by going to see him first."

She pushed her hair out of her eyes and twisted
it back on her head. Cade had the urge to touch the
wayward strands, but he made himself pack up the
rest of the boxes.

"Don't beat yourself up. You were excited about getting started." Cade did his best to be encouraging.

"Don't pander to me, Cade. I made a mistake. A
rookie one, I'm sure. Now I need to backtrack and
do what I should have done this morning when I
got here."

"That's a good idea." Cade ignored her comment about pandering. He had a feeling she wouldn't believe him if he tried to explain that wasn't what he meant to do. "If he didn't take the files, then that's a clue for us. Don't you think?"

Patience pursed her lips. "Definitely. I'll stop by the station and ask him, but first I need a shower. I feel like I have ten layers of dust on me and I haven't even checked into the B and B yet."

The image of Patience naked with warm water and soap sluicing down her body was almost more than he could take. Cade returned the boxes to where they found them. "You said you were staying at the B and B?"

"Yes. Staying at a B and B takes me into the life of the townspeople, which is helpful when you're trying to understand the local culture. You said you were hanging around for a few weeks, where are you staying?"

"Same place, just around the corner from the diner."

A small smile turned up the edges of her mouth. Could she possibly be happy about staying in the B and B with him? "If you want to follow me, my truck is across the street."

"Sure." She glanced up but there was no trace of the smile he'd seen there.

As they rolled up in front of the B and B, Cade jumped out to help her with her bag.

"It's okay," she said refusing to let go of the suitcase.

"Trust me, I need you to let me do this. When we get inside you'll understand."

She gave him a curious look but relinquished the bag. "Why?"

Holding open the door, Cade ushered her in carrying both of their bags.

"My stars, if it isn't my errant grandson come home, and with a woman." His grandmother held her hand to her heart. "Are there any great-grandbabies out there for me to hold?"

Dressed in her jeans, denim shirt and cowboy boots, GG hadn't changed a bit. Her long white hair was tied in a ponytail, and she wore the silver belt buckle she'd won bull riding forty years ago. She'd always been a woman before her time.

Cade scooped her up in a big hug, and she planted a kiss on his cheek. "Missed you," he said as he put her down.

After his mom died, his grandmother was the one person in the world who kept him grounded. She was the reason he went to college and why he didn't give up when the chips were down. He owed everything to her.

She slapped his shoulder. "Now who is this beauty you brought in with you?"

"Hi, I'm Patience Clark." She held her hand out to his grandmother.

"Well, you are as pretty as they come," his

grandmother said. "I'm Dorothy Randall, this one's grandma, and I own this money pit." She winked. "Everyone calls me GG. Now, how did you meet my grandson?"

Cade knew what he would say would ruin his grandmother's good mood, but it had to be done. "GG, she's the woman who discovered what happened to Dad. She's helping the sheriff with the investigation." The last bit came out hoarse with emotion. He still had a hard time believing what had happened to his father.

GG pressed her lips together and sniffed once. No tears were shed. It wasn't her way. Then she hugged a surprised Patience.

"Bless you child for bringing my son back home to me. People been throwing tacks at his reputation ever since he disappeared and now they're all ashamed. I knew my boy wouldn't run off. I just knew it."

Patience cleared her throat. "Thank you for letting me stay here," she said as she changed the subject. "I'm not fond of motels, or even hotels, for that matter. You have a lovely home here."

His grandmother let go of her and headed behind the front desk in the lounge area. "Damn, money pit. Hailstorm two weeks ago did some damage to the roof, and the toilet is running in room six where you're staying tonight." She pointed at Cade. "You'll have to jiggle the handle."

Cade smiled. That was her way of saying he

needed to fix the roof and the toilets, and he didn't mind a bit. "I'll make a run to Tom's Hardware later and pick up what we need."

"I've got Patience in room five, the rooms are adjoining. Is that going to be a problem?" GG had a twinkle in her eye. Was it that obvious he liked the beautiful blonde next to him? Nothing much ever made it past GG.

He noticed her erasing the fact that she'd originally had Patience in room one, at the other end of the hall. He couldn't help but laugh to himself. The woman never stopped.

Patience smiled sweetly. "No, I don't mind." She'd missed GG's intimation and for that he was grateful.

"I'll take her bags up and show her the ropes." He paused. "Is that chicken and dumplings I smell?"

"Might be, but they won't be ready until six. Ya'll look like you've been rolling around in a dusty field. Maybe you ought to clean up?"

"Oh, yes," Patience said. Once again missing his grandmother's double meaning. "We've been in the basement of the courthouse. If you don't mind my saying, it's very dirty down there. The town should better preserve its history."

"Ha, I'll have to talk to the mayor about that," GG said as she chuckled.

Cade laughed as he pulled the bags upstairs and motioned for Patience to follow him.

"What's so funny?" she asked as they walked along the second floor hallway.

"GG is the mayor."

PATIENCE FACE-PALMED HERSELF. "Great, I've insulted your grandmother who is one of the loveliest people I've ever met."

Cade took the key GG had given him and opened the door. "Nah, she thought it was funny. And I bet the next time we go down to the courthouse basement it will be clean as can be. This is your room," he said as he opened the door.

Patience walked in front of him and gave out a small gasp. "It's beautiful." The walls were painted a soft cornflower-blue, and everything else was white, the furniture, comforter and linens, even the vase holding the colorful bouquet of flowers on the small nightstand.

"She's a tough old broad, but she does have a knack for turning places into homes," Cade said. "Where would you like your suitcase?"

"If you don't mind, by the bathroom would be great. Thanks for carrying everything up." She suddenly felt awkward. The room was large, but with Cade in there it didn't seem like it.

"No problem. So I guess I'll meet you downstairs in a half hour?"

"Uh-huh," she said.

Cade shut her door to the hallway and then walked

through one that adjoined their rooms. He smiled as he closed the door.

Patience fanned herself. The man did strange things to her body without ever even touching her. Unzipping her suitcase she pulled out her toiletries and clean clothes.

In the bathroom, she stripped off her dirty clothes and was about to turn on the shower when she heard someone singing. The voice was rich and beautiful, and it belonged to Cade.

Delicious shivers shot down her spine. She listened for a moment before turning on the shower over the big claw-foot tub. She pulled the curtain around to keep the water from drenching the floor.

Cade was on the other side of the wall. Even with the water running she could hear his humming. Why did the man affect her so?

It's an infatuation.

How long has it been since you've been on a date? Too long.

Patience showered quickly, turning on a cold blast of water at the end to send her traitorous body a message. She had to focus on what was most important—the case. With the towel wrapped around her she stepped out just as her phone rang.

It was the sheriff.

"Dr. Clark, heard you were over at the courthouse this afternoon, thought I'd check up on you."

"Thanks, Sheriff. I should have come to see

you first. Do you have a minute for me to ask you something?"

"Certainly. What's up?"

She told him about the courthouse. "I was wondering if you might have the files? If so, we'd like to come pick them up."

"Sorry, I haven't seen them, but that is curious. You checked several boxes and those were the only ones you found missing?"

"Yes," she said as she shimmied into her panties.

"I did some digging myself. Joseph Randall, Cade's father, was the water commissioner back then, but he also worked in the deeds department. At the time, our courthouse was a small operation and everyone helped out when necessary."

"Water commissioner? I'd imagine water's a big deal around here, where there are so many ranches."

"Yep," he said. "You know, those missing files may be in a storage facility outside of town. The old courthouse was a mess five years ago and they moved a lot of stuff out. I'll check into it and let you know."

Before returning to search the records she figured she should speak with Cade's grandmother to get some background about her son's business as the water commissioner.

Well, I'm learning as I go.

Now, grilling the woman wouldn't be her best option. Patience wasn't always known for her tact, but she knew she needed to approach Dorothy with kindness. Maybe she could ask about Cade as a child and what he was like before his father disappeared.

She stared at herself in the mirror for a moment. *You have to be patient.* What was it Katie had told her? That one sentence could change the entire way one looked at a case. She needed to keep her ears open and talk as casually as possible with those involved. And not push too hard for answers. People clammed up that way, Katie had reminded her.

Her friends often joked that her name was a misnomer. In her lab, Patience always took her time, but when it came to the rest of her life—well, she had a way of being abrupt and saying exactly what was on her mind. She didn't have time for the games people often played. And to be honest she didn't understand them. Unfortunately, from what her friends had warned, game play was a part of solving cases. Often a cat-and-mouse game.

Given what she'd seen already, her direct way wouldn't work to her advantage here.

There was a knock on the door. "Are you ready?" Cade asked.

She quickly slipped on her T-shirt. "Yes, I'll meet you downstairs." Her mind shifted to the sound of his beautiful voice as he'd been singing.

She turned toward the shower wondering if she might need another cold spray. Patience was dressed, but she wasn't sure about being ready for whatever it was Cade might offer her.

4

"I HAVE TO SOLVE THIS CASE quickly and get out of this town," Patience said as they left the B and B and stepped onto the sidewalk. She picked up speed as she hit the concrete for their walk to the courthouse.

Cade glanced at her sharply. "Why? I thought you enjoyed dinner. Did GG say something while I was upstairs?"

Laying a hand on his arm, she smiled. "No, I adore her. The food was incredible, but that's why. A few more days of eating like this, and you'll have to roll me out of town. I thought I might pop the zipper on my jeans before we even finished the meal."

Your jeans look just fine. The way they hugged her slightly rounded behind and showed off her legs.

Cade stopped. He shouldn't be thinking like this. He had to concentrate, get back to Austin. The merger.

Taking her hand, he tucked it in the crook of his

elbow. He had to confess he was relieved by her joking about leaving town. Throughout dinner she'd talked mainly to GG, and Patience had charmed them with her openness and honesty.

"I love food, too," Cade said honestly. "I'm usually a nut about eating healthy and exercise. Of course, all that flies out the window when I smell my grandmother's cooking. But I plan to work it all off at the ranch this trip."

"I'd like to see it."

"The ranch?"

She nodded. "I've never been to a real working ranch."

"Sure, although I don't exactly have it working just yet. But my foreman and I are at least making some headway. I'll take you out there anytime you want to go. But no judgments. The old house where I spent part of my childhood looks pretty beat-up on the outside, though the inside really isn't so bad."

The house had been in the family for more than eighty years, and his grandmother and all her sisters and brothers had been born there. His father had also been born and raised in the house.

Cade had to clear this throat. His father was the good man his grandmother always claimed him to be. She and Cade's mother were the only people in town who had believed his father hadn't run off with some woman.

"Cade?"

"What?"

Cocking her head, Patience watched him carefully with those beautiful green eyes of hers. "You look upset."

He forced a smile. "Sorry, I was thinking about my dad. His reputation was maligned by most of the town. Eventually, I even believed the rumors. Now I feel so guilty for all the mean words I said about him. I hated him for so long and now—"

"You were a kid, that couldn't have been easy."

"No, for the first couple of months I caused my mom and grandmother so much grief. Fistfights every day, and I was small so I came home with a lot of black eyes."

"You were defending your family and I find that quite honorable."

Cade took a deep interest in the dust sprinkling the top of his boots. There was absolutely nothing honorable about the thoughts he'd had about his dad. "Every night I prayed he'd come home to us. Then after six months, I just gave up on him."

"Like I said before you were—" Patience was interrupted by a loud shriek and then a string of foul words.

"Sounds like that came from the park." Cade pulled her along with him as he went to investigate the source. They rounded the corner by Tom's Hardware Store and found the park crowded with people working on various booths.

"What is all this?" Patience asked as they walked

down the path to where the booths were being built.

"The town is getting ready for the annual Firefly Festival," Cade answered. "Andy was that you howling like a dog in heat?" he joked with his old friend.

Andy held a towel around his fingers and from the hammer on the ground Cade knew exactly what had happened.

"Well, Mr. Big Man is gracing us with his presence." With his good hand he punched Cade in the shoulder. "Great to see ya."

"Same here." Cade smiled at his friend. He hadn't seen him since they'd had drinks a year ago when Andy had come to Austin for an auction. He and his wife, Celia, who had been one of their high school friends, owned the antique shop on the square in downtown Phosphor.

"Where is your better half? I thought she banned you from all tools, especially hammers and saws."

Andy hung his head. "Why do you have to make me look bad in front of your lady friend? And why—" he faced Patience "—is someone as beautiful as you hanging out with this runt?"

She laughed and held out her hand. "I'm Patience."

Andy held out his left hand for an awkward shake. "Nice to meet you."

"Patience is investigating my dad's case."

Andy's face grew solemn. "I heard about that. I'm

sorry. I can't imagine what you've been going through and—" Cade knew Andy must have realized he'd said too much in front of Patience.

"Sorry," he said. "My mouth doesn't work any better than my hands. But I'm glad you finally have the truth. If I can help find the bastard who killed him, you know I'm all in."

Cade couldn't have asked for a better friend, and he felt a world of guilt for letting so much time pass since their last meeting. "I appreciate the offer. I really do. So where is that wife of yours?"

"You just missed her. I was worried she was getting tired and she looked a little pale."

Cade frowned. "Is she sick?"

Andy's face widened into the biggest smile Cade had ever seen. "Nah, she's pregnant. Five months."

Cade put a hand on Andy's shoulder. "That's one lucky kid."

His friend nodded. "Going to be one ornery little ankle-biter with Cel and I as parents. We're going to spoil the kid rotten."

"You look like the happiest man in the world," Patience said. "Congratulations."

"We'd all but given up on having our own and were looking into adopting, so it was quite a surprise." Andy shook his head. "Celia's about to bust at the seams she's so happy." He rolled his eyes. "Don't tell her I said anything about busting out. She's very self-conscious about her weight, but I think she looks more beautiful than ever." Andy flexed his injured hand.

"What were you trying to do?" Cade picked up the hammer from the ground where his friend had tossed it.

"I thought I'd better get some supports up for the booth, before the storm got here, didn't want the booth flying around like Dorothy's house in the *Wizard of Oz*. Figured I could handle three or four two-by-fours."

Cade turned to Patience. "I'm going to take a few minutes and help him out."

She smiled. "I'll help him pack up the rest of the tools."

"Now that's right nice of both of you," Andy said.

"No problem. I've been eating Cade's grandmother's food and I feel like I've gone up two jean sizes in an hour."

Andy laughed.

Cade picked up the boards and a sack of nails. As he added the supports and fixed the counter in front, he listened to his friend and Patience chat.

He couldn't believe his friend was going to be a father, though he hadn't lied. Andy and Celia would be incredible parents. They were loyal, loving, funny and smart. And some of the best people he knew.

Cade often invited them to come up to his house on Lake Austin for laid-back weekends. But the past year… He hadn't made time for anyone, not even his family. He couldn't remember the last time he'd been on a date.

That had to be why he was so into Patience. It had been a while since he'd been with a woman—a long while.

Patience stacked the rest of the boards while Andy searched for loose nails. They talked back and forth as if they had been friends for years. Cade felt the same way about her and secretly it pleased him.

Why?

Oh, I think you know exactly why.

Patience was beautiful and smart, and…

Yep. He was in trouble.

BACK IN HER ROOM, Patience brushed out her hair and changed into an oversize T-shirt. She sat down on the edge of the bed and opened her laptop. She was so far behind on email it was ridiculous. She replied to the ones that were necessary and then perused her early information on the Randall case.

A noise from the next room made her jump. Then she realized it was Cade fixing the toilet. A wrench or some tool must have thudded on the wooden floor. There was something about a man who was good with tools. More than once she had caught herself catching a peek at his hard muscles as he worked on the booth for his friend.

Here was this multimillionaire, known as a shark in the business world, who thought nothing of picking up a hammer to help a friend.

Her opinion of him had changed so much since they first met. He was a caring, loving grandson and friend. She could tell by the way he communicated with Andy that there was a deep connection there. And honestly, a man didn't have friends like Andy if he wasn't good-hearted.

Patience checked herself. She shouldn't care anything about the man's personal life. She was here to solve a case, and that's where her focus needed to be. It was hard to separate the man from the work, especially when he was right next door. She didn't date much, but even she was aware of how hard it was to find a man like Cade Randall.

He'd been so passionate about his ranch, and she'd noticed he smiled more when he discussed what he wanted to do with the place he called the Triple Dare. The idea of restoring the ranch had been something Cade had thought about for a long time.

She wondered if this was some way of honoring his father or making up for the years he'd been so bitter about his dad's disappearance.

Patience knew about being bitter and losing someone you loved. There wasn't a day she didn't think about the soul-sucking moment when her life had forever changed.

5

CADE'S FIRST THOUGHT WHEN he sat straight up in bed was that someone was crying. Rain beat down on the roof, and he wondered if maybe that was what he'd heard. There was another sob. Taking a moment to get his bearings he determined the noise had come from Patience's room.

Patience called out to someone. He couldn't hear the name, but the sob behind it was clear. The gut-wrenching sadness of the sound tore at him. Something was terribly wrong.

After sliding on his jeans, he knocked on the door separating their room.

She didn't answer.

He heard another soft sob.

"Patience?" He opened the door. She was twisted in her sheets. "Hey, are you okay?"

"Jeremy… I'm sorry. I'm so sorry. Please come home."

Who was Jeremy? A pang of jealousy hit him.

He knelt at the bedside and saw she was sound asleep but in the middle of some kind of nightmare. "Patience." He softly pressed his hand to her cheek.

"Hey, wake up," he said softly. But the tears continued to flow.

Each sob constricted his heart. He couldn't stand to see her this way. "Patience, come on, I need you to wake up." This time he lightly jostled her shoulder and her eyes fluttered open.

"Cade?"

"You were having a bad dream."

She turned to stare out the window. "I— Sometimes that happens." She cleared her throat. "I'm sorry I woke you. Please, go back to bed."

Cade smoothed a hand over her shoulder. "Don't worry. I just wanted to make sure you're all right. Do you want to talk about it?"

"No," she said. "I'm fine. Embarrassed."

"Why? It's not like you can control something like that. And we're friends. You don't have to be embarrassed with me." He meant it, though at times he had to admit he felt a little more than friendly toward her—well, way more.

"Thank you." She sniffled.

"Are you sure you don't want to talk?"

"No, I'm fine. Please go back to bed and forget this ever happened."

"Hey." He pushed a strand of hair off of her forehead. "You aren't the only one with nightmares. I've had a couple since you figured out what happened to my dad. All that boyhood trauma coming back to play." He dealt with it by pounding on a punching bag in his gym. "I don't know what upset you, but don't feel bad about it. GG always said we work things out in our dreams and usually it isn't always the fun stuff."

She glanced back at him. "I really adore that woman."

"Me, too. So, are you better?"

"I will be."

The haunted look in her eyes hadn't eased.

"I love the sound of the rain on the tin roof. It's soothing, don't you think?"

"I've never been in a house with a tin roof," she said, leaning back against the headboard.

He glanced around searching for a place to sit, this room only had one of those small white wicker benches and he knew it couldn't handle his weight.

"Do you mind if I sit on the covers over there and watch the rain through the window. It really is relaxing for me."

Cade didn't wait for her to answer him. He walked to the other side of the bed and sat on top of the covers. Propping up the pillow, he mimicked her action and leaned back against the headboard.

"Cade?"

Silently, he gathered her in his arms.

She hesitated, as if she were making a life or death

decision. Then she snuggled into him and he tugged a blanket up over her shoulder.

Her nearness was almost his undoing. He wanted to kiss her pain away, and the honeysuckle scent of her was enough to push him to try it.

But that wasn't what she needed.

Clearing his throat, he began, "Tomorrow, well, later today, I'm going to work on fixing the barn door out at the ranch. The structure is good, but like everything else on the property, it needs an overhaul."

Cade talked and stroked her hair until he could hear her breathing steadily. He didn't want to move for fear of disturbing her. And he convinced himself to stay through the night, in case she had another bad dream.

Yeah, keep telling yourself that, Romeo.

PATIENCE HAD A SHARP PAIN in her neck. She shrugged her shoulders as she opened her eyes. There was a pair of strong jean-clad thighs in front of her.

Sitting up she found Cade staring at her with a warm smile on his face. "Morning."

The night before came rushing back to her and she almost cringed when she realized what she'd done. "Hi," the word came out a whisper. A little cough escaped her throat. "Did you get any sleep?"

"A couple of hours. That's all I need." There was something in his eyes that she couldn't read. Her usual lack of understanding human emotion was nothing less than frustrating at times like these.

She sat up on her knees accidentally touching his thigh as she did so.

He jerked slightly as if her touch repulsed him.

"Sorry. For—that and for everything," she said quickly. "You were so sweet to stay with me." She leaned forward to grab her pillow as he lifted his head. Their lips touched.

Before she could pull back, his mouth moved against hers, challenging and taking everything she had to give. She tried analyzing what was happening, but his tongue slid across hers and it was Patience who lost her breath. The man was delicious.

What are you doing?

She had the sense to push away and sat back.

Patience's cheeks were hot and she knew they must be a dark shade of pink. "That was nice."

"Nice?" One eyebrow went up.

"Yes, and unexpected," she added.

"Yes, unexpected is a good way of stating it." His hand caressed her cheek. "I'd be liar if I said I was disappointed."

"Yeah, I'd be liar if I said that, too."

The man looked at her as if ready to eat her up, and she was more than happy to be his dish. For a second she thought he might reach for her, but he rolled off the bed.

"Is there something wrong?" she asked.

"No, I'm checking for leaks. GG said the roof was leaking and we had a good soaking rain last night, thought I'd better see if there was water damage."

Why wouldn't he look at her? Had she done something to turn him off?

"Oh," she said.

"I'd better check the other rooms."

Patience had offended him. She tried to think back to what happened directly after the kiss, but she couldn't think of anything.

He stepped through the doorway connecting their rooms, calling to her, "What do you have planned today?"

"I—am going out to the crime scene. I want to make sure we haven't missed anything." She was slightly befuddled that he even cared. He acted as if he wanted to get way from her.

"I still don't understand how there could be evidence there. The weather's rough here, it would have been washed away long ago. And I thought you were a forensic anthropologist, not an archaeologist."

"I am, but I spent a good part of my youth helping my dad on various digs. You're also right about the weather, and there are insects, too, besides the erosion that can disrupt a crime scene. However, as I've learned, the land can hold on to some surprising things. I won't know unless I go over the surrounding area myself."

"Never thought of it like that," Cade said. "So what time are you leaving?"

"After breakfast. Why?"

"I'll come with you, I don't want you going out there alone."

Her eyebrow rose this time. "I'm a big girl, Cade, I don't need a chaperone."

"I know, but I want to be there, okay? I need to go to the store so if you can hold off until about ten or so, I'd appreciate it."

"Sure," she said lightly.

Something flashed in his eyes. That she wanted him so much was clouding her judgment. This kind of complication she didn't need. Focus was the name of the game.

When you solve the case, then you can taste him again.

And yet...

Her traitorous body might die if it had to wait too long. Never had she craved a man's touch like she did his.

Cade Randall was an addictive drug, one that she'd have to take in small doses if she was going to survive.

6

CADE ENJOYED STUDYING PATIENCE as she worked. Painstakingly methodical, she searched through the dirt and landscape looking for anything that could give her a clue. Initially he'd helped her by going thirty feet out walking in circles until he spiraled back to the old oak where the sheriff found his father's remains.

Cade would have given up an hour ago, but Patience kept at it. Right now she was near the grove of trees to the west. She stooped down to pick up something shiny with the tweezers she carried and put it in one of the evidence bags she carried in her pocket.

She was confident and self-assured and he didn't doubt that she knew exactly what she was doing. Her fragility from the night before was gone, except perhaps a slight darkening under her eyes. As he held her in his arms the previous night, it had shocked him when he realized he'd do anything to protect her. By the morning he'd decided it was merely a manly instinct and one that he would have felt about any woman in a similar circumstance.

Using a large stick she poked into the underbrush around a group of trees. About the time he was worried she'd run into a snake, she jumped back.

Cade hopped off the truck. "What is it?"

She waved him away. "It's okay, just a rattlesnake."

"Just?"

"He surprised me, well, I'm pretty sure I surprised him first," she said as she walked over to him. Most of the women, hell, a good portion of the men he knew would have run screaming.

"I run into creatures all the time when I'm out in the field. I try to be respectful since I'm in their territory, but every once in a while I make a mistake."

"You amaze me." Cade meant the words.

"Why is that?" She took a swig of water from her bottle.

"That you don't have a clue cracks me up. I saw you pick something up before the snake surprised you."

She pulled the package out of her pocket. When she held it up his breath caught in his chest. "That's—" The words wouldn't come.

"Did this belong to your father?"

Cade didn't trust his voice. He took the package

from her so he could read the inscription. "Love's enough" was written inside the simple gold band. He held his father's wedding ring. When they were first married, his parents didn't have much money and his mother always told him that love was enough to see them through.

Anger burned in Cade's gut. What happened to his father hit him like a two-ton truck. Leaving the ring on the tailgate, he walked away.

The tiny piece of metal forced Cade to think about everything he and his family lost. He wanted to scream. Pain shot through him at how all their lives had been ruined.

Cade dropped to his knees. The emotions roiled inside him. All the hate he'd felt toward his father was replaced by a desperate need for his killer to be brought to justice.

There was also the heart-sinking guilt. He might have only been seven when his father disappeared, but Cade should have known. His dad was a good man.

Memories of fishing on the river, and helping his father gather hay on the weekends flooded his mind. Sitting in his dad's lap so Cade could feel as if he was driving the tractor. His first solo ride on a horse. After only a few times around the ring he'd fallen off. "You can give up and never ride again," his father had said gently, "or you can get back on that horse and show him who is boss. I believe in you, son, and I'm proud of you, no matter what you decide." Cade had hauled himself onto the horse and ridden until his mom had called them in for dinner. That night he'd caught his dad looking at him at the dinner table. He remembered the pride in his father's eyes.

Cade's hands splayed on his thighs and he gulped for air. Tears burned the rims of his eyes, but he was a proud man and refused to let them fall.

"I'll kill whoever did this," he vowed.

"I wouldn't blame you," Patience said, as she tentatively placed a hand on his shoulder.

Her touch was a salve. It soothed his conscience in a way he'd never expected.

"The ring made it real," she said, filling the silence. "For the first time in years."

Cade continued to stare at the ground. The idea that she perhaps had shared his kind of pain calmed him. The need to comfort her grew stronger than his anger and grief.

"I'm sorry. It isn't fair," she said. "And if it means anything, I'd probably help you kill whoever did this to you." Cade heard a hint of anger in her voice and pushed himself off the ground to stand before her.

"I envy you in a way." Her voice caught.

A single tear slid down her cheek. How could she possibly envy the fact his father had been murdered?

"Envy?" he asked her.

She shook her head, and pushed the tear away with a fist. "I'm sorry. I know that sounds terrible. I just meant, at least you know what happened to him. As tough as it is, you no longer have to wonder why he disappeared. I'm not sure I'll ever know what happened to Jeremy."

"Can I ask who he is?" Cade wasn't at all sure he wanted to know, but he could tell she was ready to talk. He'd do anything to get his mind off his own troubles.

"He's— It's not important right now," she said, her voice raw with emotion. She bit her lip and Cade could see she fought for control.

"Tell me about him." He didn't let go of her arm. He watched as fear and then what looked like remorse played over her face.

"This isn't about me, Cade," she said, her voice hoarse. "It's about you. We need to get to town and show the sheriff what I found."

Cade didn't let go of her. Instead, he led her to the tailgate of the truck and lifted her onto it. Then he sat down beside her.

"How is it you can relate to all this?"

Patience's head dipped down, as if she were trying to hide her pain from him. Cade put an arm around her shoulders. When he touched her, she took in a deep shuddering breath and shook her head. This was a deep sorrow born of years of pain. He knew because he'd felt the same way.

"Please?" he asked again.

"Jeremy is my brother," she finally answered.

Scooting closer to him she snapped her arms around his body as if she were hanging on to an emotional anchor. He tightened his hold.

"When I was thirteen he was six. During the school years my father taught at the university in town, and summers we would go with him on expeditions. Every day I walked Jeremy home from school. He had to wait a half hour for me to get out, but my school was across the street so he'd sit on the steps and wait for me. But one day he wasn't there.

"At first I was so mad at him for running off. I checked the playground and then went over to his school. His teacher, Mrs. Glade, saw how worried I was and she gathered some others to help look for him. They checked the school, and I ran to the homes of his two best friends. The last time they'd seen him, he'd been on the steps of my school. That's when I called my dad." Her voice trembled when she mentioned her father.

She glanced up at him, and the pain in her eyes took Cade's breath away. The confident, self-assured woman was once again a little girl.

"The police were called in and a search team. We combed the neighborhood, but it was as if he'd just disappeared. The last time anyone had seen him, he'd been on those damn steps right where he was supposed to be."

The tears flowed now and Cade dug around in his pocket for his bandana. Patience didn't seem to be aware of the tears. He blotted them away for her, cursing himself now for asking about Jeremy.

"There were statewide and then nationwide searches. Still, the police didn't have a single lead. My father took a year's leave of absence and did nothing but look for my brother. Our mother had died of cancer when Jeremy was four and he couldn't stand the idea of losing another family member.

"For a long time I blamed myself. That day I'd lingered at my locker to talk with a boy that I liked. I wondered if I'd been on time, would Jeremy have been there waiting for me? Maybe because I was a little bit late he left and decided to walk home and that's when someone kidnapped him."

"You can't believe it was your fault," Cade pushed her hair behind her ears. "You were little more than a child yourself. Whoever took your brother is to blame, not you."

She coughed a little and Cade handed her the bandana.

"I know that's true, but there's a part of me that will never let go of the feeling that I maybe could have done something. I imagine the most horrible things happened to him. My father never blamed me. He told me he always believed someone saw what a wonderful little boy Jeremy was, and they gave him a good home. But the world doesn't work that way. I knew that even back then.

"At the end of the year Jeremy went missing, my

dad pulled me out of public school. He had me tutored privately and we traveled the world. He never let me out of his sight. It wasn't until I went to university that he finally let go. Even now he texts me once a day, every day, even though he's remarried and has my stepbrothers to worry about."

"Well, you never know, your father might be right about someone kind kidnapping your brother. We hear stories about women who will do anything to have a child. Have you ever used your resources at Stonegate to find him?"

Patience shrugged. "I thought about it a couple of times, but—"

"What?"

"What if we do find a lead? What if I get my hopes up and we find out the worst? Sometimes I believe not knowing is easier."

"I'm surprised to hear you say that. When you took on my dad's case the first thing you said was he deserved to rest in peace. That meant finding out what had happened to him."

She shoved him gently. "This is not the time for you to be throwing my words back at me, Cade."

"Ha, I happen to know this hardheaded woman who would do anything to find out what happened to my dad. I think she should also put some of those skills to use for her own cause. Have you ever told any of your friends at Stonegate?"

She sighed. "No. I've never told anyone but you."

Cade's chest tightened. "I'm honored. And yet, I think you need to at least try, Patience. Your brother deserves the same as my dad. As hard as it has been for me the last two weeks, I wouldn't trade knowing my father was a good man for anything. I at least have some closure, even if it isn't the ideal situation. You deserve the same. He may be alive somewhere wondering where you are."

"Or I could find out he's dead."

"Yes, that is a possibility," Cade said carefully, "but at least you would know."

They sat in silence for several moments and his thoughts ran the gamut. Cade wanted to take the pain away from her. He had financial resources that could help her search. The merger had made him a wealthy man several times over and if her friends wouldn't help her for free, he'd pay them, too.

You're in deep.

Maybe too deep.

Cade kissed the top of her head and she lifted her face to him.

"I need something from you, Cade, and I'm embarrassed to ask," she said softly.

"Tell me. I'll do anything for you, Patience."

"Make love to me, Cade. Now. Help me forget."

Cade watched her for a few seconds and saw the need in her eyes.

"Please don't make me beg."

His hand slipped around the back of her neck as

his lips descended on hers with a ferocity he fought to control. She wanted him, and though somewhere in his mind he knew he might be taking advantage of the situation the feel of her pressed against him overrode any reason he still might have had.

He'd make her beg, but not for comfort.

7

PATIENCE'S MIND WHIRLED with the sensations of Cade's touch as he shifted closer to her on the tailgate. With every brush of his fingers and kiss from his warm lips the painful memories dulled. She allowed herself to be consumed by passion and when he kissed her again, she felt as though she'd come home.

She couldn't get enough of him. The soft glide of his caress whispered over her with reassurance. He was her sanctuary and the more they touched the more she relaxed and her troubles seemed so distant.

When his hand brushed her breast she pushed herself more fully into his palm. He squeezed her and then moved to her other breast repeating his machinations. Patience's desire surged into overdrive. She wanted to feel him inside of her.

She reached down to feel the length of him, but he

gently pushed her hand away. "I'm barely in control as it is," he murmured against her lips.

"I don't want us to be in control right now," she said honestly.

Their kisses intensified to the point where everything became blurred as she lost focus. Cade pulled away for a second and she moaned her disappointment.

Pulling himself up onto the truck, he grabbed a blanket from the toolbox and spread it over the truck bed. Patience crawled onto the blanket. They watched each other for a moment, and then she leaned down to tug off one cowboy boot and then the other.

Cade followed her motions. She slid her jeans down and slipped off her T-shirt leaving nothing but a pink lacy bra and panties.

Hunger grew in his eyes and a slight flush tinged her body when she realized that look was for her. Well, the huge tent in his gray boxers was also a big clue. She positioned herself on the blanket and reached up to him.

"You're so beautiful."

"I don't need flattery, only you," she said.

"But you are the most beautiful woman I've ever met."

Her heart fluttered and Patience was sure her face had turned a lovely shade of fuchsia. No one called her beautiful. She was stuck-up, frigid and cold—she'd heard those words plenty of times. But Cade didn't see her that way. Heat bloomed within her.

He knelt down. "Are you sure?" The naked desire in his eyes heated her body to the core.

She reached for him again.

Cade lay down beside her. As his tongue pushed between her teeth, his hand moved up and down her thigh. He reached the top of her panties and pushed them down her legs. When his fingers touched her heat she arched. He found the nub filled with nerves and his hand soon had her panting.

"Cade, please," she begged.

"Please, what?"

"I need you inside me now."

His hand didn't stop.

Patience grabbed the blanket as she cried out her orgasm. "Please, now. Please."

Cade removed his boxers, then reached into his jeans pocket to pull out a foil packet. She didn't know when he'd put it there, but she was grateful. That he'd planned ahead of time meant their thoughts had been on the same path. He wanted her, and that gave her a new sense of power.

She took the packet from him and rolled the condom over the length of him. As she guided him into her, she couldn't help extending her hand up and down his hardness.

"If you don't let go, this will end a lot faster than either of us wants it to," Cade warned, as he nibbled her ear.

She instantly let go.

"I want to take it slow with you, hon."

She shook her head digging her fingernails into his shoulders. "No. Now," she said. "Later we can do it slow. Right now I need you to fill me up, Cade."

Desire flashed in his eyes. He was so thick that she worried for a split second, but her body opened to him as if it had been waiting forever. He met her furious pace thrust for thrust.

She shuddered with an orgasm and begged him to come with her, but he wasn't finished with her yet.

Cade's hips moved even faster. Her body arched as she reached the precipice and finally he gave her that final release. With her legs wrapped around his waist, she heard him moan, although it sounded as if it were coming from a long distance away. Her body was liquid fire.

"Cade," she cried out.

"Patience," he groaned out her name as he emptied himself inside of her.

For a moment she wasn't sure she was still on planet Earth.

Cade collapsed on top of her. "I'd planned to take that a little slower." He kissed her chin.

"That isn't what I wanted," she said as she ran her fingers through his hair. "It seems wrong to say thank you, but that, well, that was nothing short of mind-blowing."

He chuckled. "I feel like I should be the one saying thanks, you are something else."

Patience rolled onto her side to face him. "I wanted you to make love to me this morning, but you ran off."

He smoothed a hand up and down her arm and smiled. "I wanted the same thing, but you'd had a tough night and I didn't feel right taking advantage of you."

"You wouldn't have been."

"If it helps, I was having a really hard time keeping my hands off of you. And when I say hard…"

This time she laughed. "Oh." *That's why he had his back to me when he walked to the next room.*

The sun beat down on them, and Patience realized she was about to get sunburned in places that had never seen its rays. "I guess I should get back to the courthouse," she said as she shook out her clothes. "And I still need to talk to the sheriff."

Cade was dressing, too. "While you talk to the sheriff, I'll run to the hardware store and then I can help you at the courthouse. But if the records are missing, isn't it kind of a mute point?"

Patience frowned. "No, I had a message from my friends at Stonegate this morning. From what they said, this kind of stuff gets misfiled all the time. So I need to go through more of the boxes."

"We'll go through them." He leaned over and kissed her.

"Okay."

He held her close and deepened the kiss, and she lost herself in him once again.

THE SHERIFF WASN'T IN HIS office, so Cade and Patience decided to go straight to the courthouse. Of course he'd driven her back to town in a daze. Making love with her had helped him out of one of his darkest moods, but the way she'd pinned him with that gaze of hers as she climaxed wasn't something he would forget anytime soon.

They'd been quiet on the ride to town, both of them seemingly distracted by their own thoughts. When he wasn't remembering what they'd just done, he was thinking about his father's case. Patience finding that ring had made it all come home. No longer could he stand on the sidelines and pretend as though this was happening to someone else. More than ever he was determined to find his father's killer.

Suddenly, Patience let out a soft groan.

"What's wrong?"

She pointed to a large sign on the door. The courthouse was closed for the weekend.

"Who closes shop at noon on Thursday?"

"My guess is they want to give people time to get ready for the beginning of the festival tonight."

"Now what am I supposed to do?"

Cade's mind flashed to her naked body in the back of the truck, but he needed to stay focused. There was a lot at stake in the investigation. And now there were even more questions than answers.

"We could get some lunch and talk about what you've found so far," Cade suggested.

There was a long silence.

"I'm not really hungry right now. I'd like to get back to the B and B, talk with some of the Stonegate investigators."

Patience continued to look out the window. He'd give anything to know what she was thinking, but he also knew this wasn't the right time. She was edgy about something. "Maybe we could do a conference call. I'd like to be involved," he said as they pulled up in front of the B and B.

Patience jumped out of the vehicle quickly. "I don't think that's a good idea. Since you're a client, it's best to inform you when we actually have something. That way, you don't get your hopes up or read too much into things."

The way she said, "read too much into things" caused his jaw to harden. "Are we talking about the case or are we talking about what just happened with us?"

"Cade, I really don't have time for this."

He was around the truck before she could get to the porch steps. "Don't shut me out, Patience. Not now."

She shook her head. "Cade, I'm sorry. Listen, we're just two people who needed comfort. I'm grateful to you for that, but it can't continue. I need to concentrate on solving what happened to your father."

"So we used each other and now we move on? That's your plan?" The words sounded bitter, but he couldn't help it. What they'd shared was way more than comfort, whether she was willing to admit it or not.

"Yes. I'll see you later." She darted past him and into the B and B.

That was it; he'd finally figured it out. She was scared.

She'd said more than once that she wasn't exactly a people person—still, she could think she was a loner all she wanted, he'd been there and knew differently.

So Cade would change her mind.

8

IT WAS IMPOSSIBLE TO TELL GG no, Patience decided. She watched the older woman unpack a picnic lunch. Before she could race upstairs and get her thoughts together, GG had stopped her in the dining room of the B and B and nearly ordered her to come to the Randall family picnic. Patience had tried to make excuses—that she had work to do, which was true— but GG wouldn't hear of it. Cade had driven GG and Patience out to the lake. Most of the trip had been in silence as GG looked from one to the other with that questioning gaze of hers.

Once at the lake, Patience discovered the Randall family was loud and boisterous and she had a difficult time not succumbing to their charms. Most of them didn't live in Phosphor and had come from all over Texas to attend the Firefly Festival in town. She was usually a quiet observer in large groups, but the Randalls forced her to participate. She'd met a variety of aunts, uncles and cousins, and the anthropologist in her was fascinated by the family dynamics. They gave each other a hard time but there was also a lot of love.

"Are you thinking about the case?"

An older gentleman stood next to her and she searched her memory for his name. "I should be, but the science part of my brain is having fun watching the family dynamics here."

The older man chuckled. "I don't know about any of them being dynamic, but they're good kids."

Uncle Jake. She finally remembered his name. This probably wasn't the right time or place but, more than anything, she wanted to ask him about Cade's father. They were brothers and there was a good chance he might recall something important to the investigation. Just as she opened her mouth to ask him about the time before Joseph died, someone called out to her.

"Hey, Curly, toss me one of those beers you brought," said Logan Randall from his inner tube on the lake.

Patience reached into the cooler for the beer and tossed it to him.

"Whoa, good throw. She's on my team for the softball game," Logan announced.

"That's not happening," Cade interjected. He'd been very protective of her since they arrived. He probably thought she would feel overwhelmed and on any other day he would be right. But his cousins' good-natured ribbing made her feel welcome.

"Fight ya for her." Logan slid his expensive sunglasses up and winked at Patience. She couldn't help but laugh.

"Now, now, boys. No need to fight over fresh meat," Kent announced from his inner tube.

"Hey, watch it, Kent, or you'll find yourself down at the other end of the river where the gators like to hang out," Cade warned. "She's not meat."

Kent dipped his ball cap toward Patience. "Apologies, ma'am."

Another female at the picnic besides GG, which the woman had insisted Patience call her, was the owner of the diner, Charli. Patience tried to help the women set up the food when she arrived with Cade, but they had shooed her away so he could introduce her to the rest of the family.

Since they'd arrived, his arm seldom left her shoulders. At first she thought their lovemaking had been born out of their mutual pain, a one-time thing to comfort each another. Cade seemed to have other ideas about that. She'd wanted the man from the moment she'd met him. This kind of intimacy was new to her, and she wasn't quite sure what to make of it.

She'd dated, though not much in the last few years. But one-night stands with no emotional attachments were usually more in her comfort zone. This—well, whatever she'd shared with Cade—was different.

She glanced up to find him watching her again with a big smile on his face.

"What?"

Before he could answer, GG ordered, "Cade, you and Logan arrange picnic tables so we can all eat together."

The other men pulled their floats and inner tubes up to the sandy beach and gathered around the table.

It wasn't long before stories about the cousins, including Cade, were flowing.

Jarrod chuckled. "Hey, Cade, do you remember that time you came in with a handful of garden snakes and put them in the crisper to see if they'd hibernate? GG went to make a salad and it's the only time we've ever heard her scream."

"Critters nearly jumped from the crisper they were in such a hurry to get out." GG snickered. "Opened the drawer expecting to see celery, and you can imagine my surprise."

"I don't blame you. I don't mind snakes but to find one in the fridge would be disconcerting to say the least," Patience agreed.

"Cade spent four hours scrubbing every inch of the fridge with a toothbrush and cleanser," Logan interjected. "I think he learned his lesson about outside creatures staying outside."

Kent nodded. "Yeah, but it wasn't nearly as bad as the time Logan jumped off the roof into the pile of manure and slid into the—"

GG clapped her hands loudly interrupting Kent. "You boys hush up that talk. This is not proper dinner conversation," she said as they all sat down. Cade grabbed her hand as did Logan and then everyone bent their heads for prayer.

Patience was fond of meditation and considered herself a spiritual person. She liked that these rowdy boys settled for a quiet moment as their grandmother said a blessing.

Everyone yelled, "Amen," and that's when the real fun began. They all talked at once and the food was passed in a counterclockwise circle.

This wasn't like any picnic Patience had ever been to. The table was so full of food there was barely any room for the plates. There were three giant foil containers of barbecued brisket and ribs, along with ten different side dishes and seven pies.

"I can't believe they made all this food," she whispered to Cade.

"Just wait, with this crowd there won't be any leftovers." He piled a giant spoonful of potato salad on his plate. "We Randalls know how to eat."

The man didn't lie. If she hadn't seen it for herself, Patience wouldn't have believed it.

As soon as the last person was done, everyone stood up and cleared the table, tossing the plates into the trash and repacking the dishes. Patience tried to help, but Logan gently pushed her back onto the picnic bench. "Guests don't clean," he informed her.

Five minutes later everything was done and the tables wiped clean. Then the men went down to the lake and started tidying up all over again.

"Wow. You really do have them well trained, especially the guys," Patience said in awe.

"Firm hand is all it takes," GG said. "They lived all over the country growing up, but I had them most summers, sometimes all at once. Never had to swat a one of them, but I was always consistent. They're all good boys, my grandsons, but like most men they need some gentle guidance."

Charli laughed. "I don't know about gentle. She'd make them do chores until they fell into bed at night. They were so tired they could barely hold their heads up at the dinner table."

GG winked at her. "Well, hard work is good for a man, and look at them. They're all successful in their own way. That comes from a solid foundation."

Charli hugged her grandmother. "You definitely gave us that." She stood up. "Well, I better get back to the diner. I'm sure Rissa is cussing me out for leaving her in charge of the lunch shift on a festival Thursday."

"This might not be the best time, but, GG, can I ask you a question?" Patience spoke softly so the others couldn't hear her.

GG took her hand. "What's on your mind?"

"I need to ask you about your son, Joseph."

GG's lips became a straight line across her face, but she nodded to Patience to go ahead.

"Do you know if there was someone who might have wanted to cause him harm? Maybe he had a falling-out with someone?"

"I've been racking my brain ever since Beau told me about finding Joseph." She held on to Patience's hand a little tighter. "I'm an old woman and that was a long time ago but, to be honest, Joseph was very much his own man. If he had trouble with someone, he wouldn't have mentioned it to me and would have handled it on his own. I can tell you, even though he was my son, he could be hardheaded sometimes. Cade gets his stubbornness from his father." She paused to look out at her children and grandchildren.

Patience could see from the older woman's expression that she was recalling memories.

"I'm sorry I ruined your lovely picnic with the investigation," Patience said. "I should have waited until we were back at the B and B."

"No, girl, you are doing your job. Don't apologize to me. You know, around that time there was a bit of a scuttlebutt over the county laying down pipes for waterlines. I don't remember the details, as I wasn't the mayor back then. But I think some of the ranchers were upset because they were worried that the county might be tapping into private wells."

"Okay, well, I'll definitely look into that." Patience's gut was sending her signals again. She just wasn't sure what they meant.

"I've said my goodbyes, I'm off." Charli leaned down to give her grandmother a hug. "Oh, and I'll see you at the dance tonight." She pointed to Patience. "I promise you're going to have the time of your life."

"Dance?"

"Yes, and don't worry, you already have a date," Cade said behind her.

She twisted around on the bench so she could see him. "Funny, I don't remember anyone asking me to a dance."

"Hmm, in that case how about—" An elbow in the ribs from Cade interrupted Logan.

"Patience, will you go to the dance with me?" Cade asked formally.

Teasing him, she glanced at Logan and back at Cade as if she were trying to make a decision. Then she shrugged. "I guess so."

Logan snorted with laughter. "Doesn't sound like she's too excited about the prospect."

Cade smirked at his cousin, then smiled at her. "I guess I'll have to do my best to make sure you know just how fun a date I can be." His voice was lower and had the husky tone it had when they were making love.

Patience held up her hand so he could help her off the bench. He pulled her up to him.

"I'm looking forward to it," she said as she pushed away from his chest. "There's just one thing."

"What's that?" His face had turned serious and she knew he was worried that she was looking for a way out of the event.

"I don't know how to dance."

"SLIDE YOUR HAND AROUND TO MY belt loop, and—" Cade stopped as Patience stepped on his toes for the third time. Luckily he'd prepared for their dance lesson by wearing steel-toed boots. They were in the downstairs dining area where he'd pushed the tables and chairs back to make an impromptu dance floor. He'd already taught her an easy version of the waltz. She had rhythm, which helped, but not much experience dancing with a partner.

They were practicing the two-step, and when she stepped on his toes Cade knew it was his fault. He was so entranced by her beauty that he kept forgetting to give her the instructions. Never in his life had he been so befuddled by a woman. She seemed clueless to how gorgeous she was. It was one of the many reasons he found her so appealing.

Tonight she wore a pair of dark jeans with boots that made her legs look eleven feet long. And a wisp of a top that tied around the neck with frills down her front. The distracting part was her upper back was completely bare. Every time his hand moved across the soft skin there his jeans threatened to tent again. Twice he had had to stop and kiss her because he couldn't go a second longer without doing so.

She'd left her hair down in loose curls, and Cade

wasn't so sure he wanted to share her with anyone at the festival. In fact, more than once he'd thought about pretending to be sick or maybe even a headache so they could stay at the B and B and she could play nursemaid. It was childish, but he didn't care.

The only thing that kept him from making a complete fool of himself was that he knew his grandmother wouldn't fall for it. She'd send Logan or one of his other cousins to bring Patience to the dance, and he couldn't have that. The idea of another man dancing with her was enough to make his hands ball into fists.

Yep. He had it bad for her.

She stumbled slightly. "Maybe I should just stick to the waltz," she said as he righted her.

"You're catching on fast. The trick to this one is the same as the waltz—just let your partner guide you. But rather than going up on your toes, keep your feet flat on the ground and shuffle through the steps."

They slid across the floor again and the third time around she really did have it down. Was there anything she couldn't do?

Earlier in the afternoon, his grandmother had pulled him aside as they'd been leaving the picnic. "She's a keeper, don't be an idiot," GG warned. "And treat her with respect, ya hear me? She isn't one of them hussies you like to call arm candy. She's a real woman and if you aren't ready to take that on, there are plenty of men standing in line, I'm sure. You treat her like she's a princess. There's a sadness in that girl's eyes, and you see what you can do about taking that away."

Cade had promised he would. His grandmother had the best judgment about human beings that he'd ever known.

"Do I really have to go to this dance?" Patience asked for the third time since they'd started their lesson. She'd been stiff when the began, as if she didn't want to touch him, but the past ten minutes or so she'd relaxed.

"GG will consider it a personal insult if you don't," Cade said carefully. Patience was searching for a way out and if he made it about him, she would have run back to her room where she'd spent most of the late afternoon. He'd wanted to talk to her after the picnic, but she hadn't given him the opportunity.

"She always get her way?"

Cade chuckled. "Yes."

"I believe it. She doesn't seem to understand that I'm here working. For her. This case isn't going to solve itself."

"What you say is true," Cade interjected. "But everyone needs a little time off. You had a busy day. You found the ring and GG told me that she remembered about the debate over the town's water supply. And you spent all afternoon talking with your friends at Stonegate and tied to your laptop."

Patience paused in their dancing. "Were you spying on me?"

Cade shrugged. "I had some business calls to follow up on and work to do. The walls aren't that thick between our rooms. As I was saying before, you've been at it most of the day. You could look at the dance tonight as a way to blow off steam and get some exercise."

The music stopped. They stared at one another for a moment. Somewhere a clock chimed eight times.

"We promised your grandmother we'd be there by eight," she reminded him.

"Patience."

She placed a finger to his lips. "Not now, Cade, please. I'll go to the dance because your grandmother asked. She said most of the town turns out, so I might have a chance to observe some of those ranchers she mentioned earlier. I may even talk to a few of them. I appreciate what you're doing with the dance lessons, but it's all business tonight."

Cade wanted to argue with her, but he knew it wasn't worth it. He'd let her have this battle, knowing with confidence that he'd eventually win the war. Patience was like one of his mergers. He only needed to show her how both sides could benefit by working together.

He backed away and picked up his cowboy hat. "I was just going to say if you need me to introduce you to anyone, or if you need me to identify someone, I'm here for you."

"Oh." Her mouth formed a perfectly kissable O

and he forced himself to ignore his body's need to explore those lips. "I— Thanks," she said finally.

"After you, ma'am." He waved her toward the door and saw confusion fly across her face.

Cade didn't bother to hide his grin. He'd help with the investigation any way he could. It was just as important, maybe more so, for him to find his father's killer. But he was also determined to convince Patience that spending time with him wasn't such a bad thing. He'd succeeded as a businessman by never backing down from a challenge, by being persistent.

Patience was about to get the full Cade Randall treatment.

9

THE LOCAL LODGE HAD BEEN transformed into a sparkling spring wonderland. Everything from ficus trees to the wooden support beams had been wrapped in twinkle lights. The large central room was packed with people when Patience and Cade arrived for the dance.

"About time you two showed up," GG said when they found her at the drinks table where she refilled the iced-tea pitchers. "I was about to send out a search party to see if you two were lost." There was a glint in her eyes that looked as though GG thought they were making out before joining the party.

Whenever she was with Cade she felt like a schoolgirl with a major crush. When he'd offered to teach her how to dance, she'd been thrilled and mortified. But he had that way of making her feel comfortable, like she could do no wrong. She knew his toes would be bruised in the morning, but he never even acknowledged that she'd made a mistake or two—or twelve.

Patience's cheeks warmed and she forced herself to concentrate on the conversation.

"Told you I was teaching her how to dance," Cade reminded his grandmother as he took the heavy cooler she'd been using to refill the tea away from her.

GG grabbed the cooler back from him. "Then you kids go get on the dance floor and show them how it's done."

"Anyone ever tell you that you're a bossy old woman?" he said, kissing her cheek.

"You ever call me old again, and I'll be searching for a switch out on the old pear tree."

Cade kissed GG's cheek and then led Patience away. She wasn't afraid of anything but nerves seized her as they stood at the edge of the dance floor. "They're all so good," she said of the dancers. Young and old twirled around the dance floor as if they'd been doing it their entire lives. "I'm sure to muck it up. Why don't we just watch from here?"

"Don't be silly, you're a natural," Cade said. He'd been a very patient teacher, but she didn't relish making a fool out of herself in front of all these people. When she and Cade arrived, she hadn't failed to notice the curious glances from some of the crowd. She much preferred finding a quiet corner somewhere and leaving the dancing to the veterans.

"If you aren't going to dance with her, I'd be more than happy to—"

"Try and die, Logan," Cade interrupted him.

"Oh, now, no reason to get testy, cuz. But I can tell you that you aren't going to monopolize her all night. Uncle Rudy says he's teaching her the Shottish, and Kent is determined that she learn the Cotton-eyed Joe."

Cade gave him a go-to-hell look that made her giggle. Nervous or not, it didn't seem like she would get out of this anytime soon.

Might as well make the most of it.

"Your time is coming, Logan." She winked at him. "But I did promise this first dance to my wonderful instructor."

Before Logan could say another word, Cade had her out on the dance floor. The first few steps were a little awkward, but they found their way.

The music slowed and Cade pulled her closer clasping their hands against his heart. The small, intimate gesture registered with her from head to toe. Patience wasn't sure she would ever understand her body's response to Cade.

As hot as their lovemaking had been, there was a connection between them that had nothing to do with sex. An intimacy she had never ever experienced before.

She still couldn't wrap her mind around the fact that they'd known each other for such a short while. Their lovemaking earlier was so intense that it had scared her. She'd tried so hard to put up a wall again, protecting herself. But Cade had a way of chipping at her defenses. Like now, being in his arms, her body and heart were at war with her mind.

Her mind believing she should get over this school-girl crush and concentrate on what was most important—the case. Her heart and body, unfortunately, disagreed. Every time he touched her, her breath caught. And the way he looked at her sometimes sent her heart thumping as if she'd run a marathon.

"Are you having fun?" Cade whispered against her ear. "You have such a serious look on your face."

She thought about lying and telling him that she was thinking of the case, but it wasn't her way. "I'm trying to figure out what's going on here."

"We're at a dance and I'm holding you close because every man in this place has his eyes on you." He pulled her a little tighter as he turned the corner of the dance floor.

"I don't want a relationship, Cade."

He pulled away from her enough to where he could see her eyes. "I know. No one said anything about a relationship. We're friends."

"What about earlier?"

He seemed to catch himself before he spoke, and then he smiled. "We were comforting one another. You said so yourself. That is what friends do during a crisis."

Patience smirked. "Really?"

"That's the story. At least until you can admit we have a deeper connection."

"I'm trying to ignore it," she said under her breath.

Cade twirled her again. "For the record, this sort of thing is new to me." Cade stroked her cheek. "I don't remember a time when I've wanted a woman so bad, or felt like I could tell her anything and she would understand."

Patience's heart exploded with caring. She reached up to touch his jaw.

He leaned down to kiss her and she gave a tiny gasp of pleasure when their lips met.

Before she could resume dancing with Cade, Logan took her in his arms.

Pausing, Cade stuck an arm between them. "At least a foot, or you'll be missing your manhood by the end of the night."

Logan laughed but moved so they were a little farther apart.

"I've never seen him like this." Logan guided her around the dance floor.

"Like what?" Patience watched as Cade held out a hand to his grandmother and gave a little bow. He really was quite the charmer.

"Possessive about a woman."

She turned her attention back to Logan. "I don't think it's possessive so much as protective."

Logan snorted. "No, it's definitely possessive. Did you know he's never brought a woman to any of our family functions?"

She shrugged.

"He's genuinely jealous, look at him."

She glanced across the dance floor to find Cade studying her. She gave him a quick smile and returned her attention to Logan.

"Probably knows we're gossiping about him."

Logan laughed again. "Patience, you can't be this clueless. You are a very smart woman." Logan nodded toward Cade. "Trust me, you're off the market, Patience, at least in Phosphor." He dipped her then, which threw her off balance. If he hadn't been so strong, she would have fallen on her butt.

The song ended just in time.

Kent showed up just in time to teach her the Cotton-eyed Joe. Several dances later Logan was back. Cade had been kept busy by GG's friends.

"Are you up for one more before the band takes a break?" Logan asked.

She took a deep breath. "I could use some iced tea and a little break. Have you seen Cade?"

"He's dancing with Michele," Logan said as he handed her a plastic cup of iced tea.

Patience found him. Michele wasn't like the older women he'd been dancing with before. She was a beautiful brunette with long legs and a cropped shirt that showed off near-perfect abs.

A knot tightened in Patience's stomach when she watched the woman tug on Cade's ear with her long red fingernails. Cade gave his dance partner an affectionate look.

A wave of nausea washed over her, and she sipped her tea to help quell the rolling feeling in her stomach.

So this is what it is like to feel jealous.

She cleared her throat. "They seem comfortable with one another."

"Yeah. They were high school sweethearts. Michele went off to Denver to college and broke Cade's heart."

"Oh." An hour ago Logan had been talking about how possessive Cade was of Patience, but with this new woman in the room it didn't seem as if he cared at all. She knew how silly she was being, but she couldn't stop the hurt.

She needed to get away.

"Can you excuse me for a minute? I need to visit the ladies' room." She handed him her tea, but didn't meet his eyes.

"Sure, it's over in the corner to the right of the band."

Getting through the crowd before the tears spilled was her main objective. Luckily, even though women were crowded around the small mirror freshening their makeup, one of the stalls was open. Patience locked the door and took a steadying breath.

What in the hell is wrong with me?

There was no reason for her to be jealous. Sure, she and Cade had been intimate but she had no claim to him. More than anyone she knew that once physical needs were met, it was perfectly acceptable to walk away.

Tell that to the knot in my stomach.

If this was jealousy, she wanted no part of it.

Logan had been wrong. Cade had only been protective of her, not possessive. They had shared a fun day together, and she'd read more into it than she should have. When Cade had commented that he felt the same way, he'd probably been talking about their mutual attraction rather than some deeper connection.

What a fool she'd been.

This is what you get for going off the rails. You should be focused on your work and solving this murder.

Her friends made fun of her need for perfection. They told her life was about making mistakes if she really wanted to live.

Fine. But this kind of mistake she would never make again.

10

CADE SEARCHED THE FLOOR for Patience. He hadn't seen her since his dance with Michele. She'd looked upset while talking to Logan and had been a constant distraction for him.

"If looks could maim," Kent said beside him. "You've got that killer stare again."

Cade shrugged. "Have you seen Patience?"

"Nah. The last time I saw her she was talking to Logan."

As his name was mentioned, Logan walked up.

"Whatever it is I didn't do it," he joked but Cade noticed the smile didn't quite go to his eyes.

"What did you say to Patience that upset her?" Cade pointed a finger at him.

Logan's right eyebrow rose. "If you want to know why she's upset, maybe you should look in a mirror."

"Logan, this isn't the time for jokes. I saw her

face when she spoke with you. Tell me what happened."

"She didn't say much, but it was in confidence. I can tell you it wasn't anything *I* said or did." Logan poked a finger back at Cade. "When I said for you to look in the mirror, I meant it."

Cade shook his head. "Fine. Where the hell is she?"

"Last time I saw her, she was headed for the ladies' room," his cousin said gruffly.

"Thanks," Cade replied and left to make his way across the busy room. The band was still on a break and the auctioneer for the Friends of the Library was on stage peddling a series of art classes. The crowd was so thick, he found himself having to go completely around the room.

"Cade, where have you been? Haven't seen you all night," Deacon, his foreman at the ranch, said. "I wanted you to meet my date, Lily."

Wanting nothing more than to wave them away so he could find Patience, Cade stopped and smiled. "It's nice to meet you." He held out his hand.

Lily, who was a willowy, fresh-faced redhead, shook his hand with a great deal of strength. "I've heard a lot about you," she said. "Deacon has told me what you two are doing up at the ranch. I think it's great. If you find yourself in need of a painter, give me a call."

"A painter?"

"I do it all, exteriors, interiors, murals. And I own the new gallery around from the bakery with all kinds of crafts and artwork."

Cade liked the woman. She was direct, but he also sensed an innate kindness. Deacon deserved a good woman like her. "I saw it the other day when I came into town. Good for you on all counts. And when we get to the house, I'll definitely have Deacon give you a call. Do you have a booth at the fair?"

She nodded. "We've got a big one with pottery and everything else you can imagine."

"Great. I'll see you there."

He started to move on, but stopped as an idea formed in his head. "Actually, once we get the new barn situated we could use some help with that. Do you do that sort of thing?"

She gave him a bright smile. "Yes. I mentioned to Deacon when he took me out there the other day that it would be beautiful if you returned it to its original blue and white, to match the house. It's going to be such a picturesque place when you're done with it."

A sense of pride filled Cade. "Thanks, and I think that's a great idea. We'll talk more later. I'm sorry, but I'm looking for my date."

"Nice to meet you," she said and waved good-bye.

Cade tipped his hat before burrowing back through the crowd.

He had to find her.

STILL HIDING IN THE STALL, Patience sighed. This is why she never allowed herself to feel much. These emotions were messy and they didn't make sense. After blowing her nose and making sure that the tears hadn't messed her makeup, she was determined to walk out there and take Logan up on his offer for another dance.

After washing her hands, she freshened her lip gloss in front of the mirror, ignoring the sideways glances she received from the other women. Part of her hoped they couldn't tell she'd been crying. The other part didn't care. Patience was strong. She didn't need a man complicating her life.

Maybe she would skip the dance with Logan and go back to the B and B for a good night's rest. Maybe sleep deprivation was her problem. The nightmares about her brother had kept her from sleeping the night before and that was what caused her to act so irrationally.

Patience stepped into the hallway leading to the main room and ran straight into one of the ranchers from the diner. He hadn't confronted her, but he had been at the table with the others.

"What are you doing here?" the man spat out. "I thought with the courthouse closed you'd be on your way back to wherever you came from. Seen ya dancing with the Randall men, I guess you do like stirring up trouble. You women are all the same."

The last thing she needed right then was a confrontation.

"I'm not stirring up anything," Patience spit out through gritted teeth. The man was nothing but a bully and she refused to back down. "And I'm not sure what business it is of yours as to whom my dance partner might be."

"My friends warned you to get out of town, and yet here you are. We don't need snoops like you messing in our business. You keep running around on property that isn't yours and you might find yourself mistaken for a coyote 'round here." He leaned forward and poked her in the shoulder.

The whiskey on his breath was overwhelming and she realized this could go bad fast if she didn't do something. When he increased the pressure on her shoulder Patience's instincts kicked in and she grabbed the man's wrist and twisted it. He yelped in pain.

"I don't know why you have a problem with me," she said tightening her hold. "But if you threaten me again, or touch me, you'll have no one to blame but yourself for the harm I'll cause you. I'm trying to solve a man's murder, and frankly maybe you should move to the top of my suspect list. I'll make sure the sheriff has your name. I don't like men who pick on or threaten women, and that's something you had better remember for your own safety."

He raised his hand as if to slap her and she twisted

a little harder. "Try it again, and I'll break it, along with your knees," she said.

The man sneered and made like he was about to spit on her.

"What's going on here?"

Patience glanced to the left to see Cade surrounded by his cousins.

"I don't need your help," she said angrily.

"Did he touch you?"

"She's a damn nuisance," the rancher spat.

Cade started toward the man, when a hand pulled him back.

"No need for that, Cade, I'll take care of this," said Beau, the sheriff who had originally brought her the case. The man had a hard look in his eyes, but it wasn't for her. He was focused on the man.

"Beau, this rancher seems to have a problem with my very existence," Patience said without taking her eyes from the man. "His friends made vague threats at the diner and he threatened me again just now."

Cade growled.

The sheriff held up a hand. "Let's keep our heads, fellas. Looks like Patience has everything in hand."

"Did he touch you?" Cade angrily repeated.

She ignored him.

Beau moved forward. "You let go of him, Patience, and I'll take it from here. Looks and smells to me like Harold here has had a few too many run-ins with Mr. Wild Turkey tonight." The sheriff moved between Patience and Harold, and she stepped aside.

Still she refused to look at Cade.

She knew it was unreasonable but Patience was more upset about his dancing with an old girlfriend than the argument with Harold, which told her that she definitely wasn't thinking clearly.

"Boys, you need to let me do my job. Let's not ruin the party because of an old drunk. I'll let him sleep it off in the jail tonight and we'll talk tomorrow."

The cousins parted and let the sheriff guide Harold away.

"Ya'll go back to the dance. I need to talk to Patience," Cade said. "Thanks, boys."

This time she met his eyes. She saw nothing but concern there, and it was almost her undoing.

The cousins didn't move at first, and then Logan said, "Come on. I'm sure Patience has had enough of the Randalls for one evening."

Cade reached for her, but she stepped back.

"I'm tired. I'll see you later." She moved past him.

He caught her arm. "I'm coming with you."

She shook him off. "That isn't necessary and I want to be alone."

Patience moved quickly through the crowd in the dance hall and was grateful for the fresh air when she got outdoors.

She was finally alone. Better to nip this thing with Cade in the bud. Their afternoon together had been nothing but them comforting one another.

She had made more of the situation than was there.

It was just sex.

Yes. Some day she'd be able to convince herself of that.

11

FOR THE LIFE OF HIM, Cade couldn't figure out what had happened in the last hour that would make Patience look at him as if he was an enemy of the state.

Maybe she'd been spooked by her encounter with Harold. That man was about to find the wrong end of Cade's fist if he didn't leave her alone. Though, he had to admit, he was proud that she had the situation under control.

Now he had to figure out why she didn't want anything to do with him. He'd followed her out of the lodge, and was only about three feet behind her.

"Patience."

She stopped but didn't face him.

"Go back to the dance," she said. "I told you I want to be alone."

Yes, she was definitely angry about something.

He stood beside her, but she still refused to look at him.

"I'm not letting you walk back to the B and B by yourself. We need to talk about what happened with Harold."

She sighed heavily.

Cade thought back through the night. "I missed something somewhere. Are you upset that I didn't catch on to what was happening with Harold earlier? I'm sorry. I was trying my best to get to you, but Michele was reminiscing about—"

She stiffened when he mentioned Michele. Could she possibly be jealous? No, Logan certainly would have explained the situation to her. Unless—

He had been an idiot.

Patience walked toward the B and B and he stayed beside her.

When they reached the porch of the B and B he touched her arm gently and turned her around to face him. She continued to look past his shoulder.

"Patience, please. If I could have found you beforehand I would have told you about Michele. You need to know that. I only have eyes for one woman, and that's you."

He slowly caressed her jawline.

She recoiled from his touch. "That's the point. It shouldn't matter who you dance with or what you do. We've only known each other for a couple of days. You're free to do whatever you want, Cade."

"No, Patience, I'm far from free. I'm so wrapped

up in you it's scaring the hell out of me. But I'm not about to let fear get in the way of how I feel about you. I don't care how long we've known each other. You feel it, too, you told me on the dance floor."

"I don't know what I feel. It's too much, too fast," she said with such anguish that he gently pulled her to him.

"Hey, if it's going too fast just say the word. We can back off. Whatever you want, Patience, really. I'm willing to do what it takes."

"This is why I don't get involved with people," she said against his chest. "I don't understand human emotions. I just don't. I was actually jealous of that woman tonight. It isn't logical. And I'm always logical."

Cade hid his grin from her. He understood her confusion. Hell, he had no idea what was happening between them, either, but he did know he had to be with her.

"I don't know a lot about relationships, either," he said honestly. "In the past five years I've seldom dated. But I do know that what we share, well, it's different."

"That's crazy," she whispered.

"True. Maybe we can't define what is happening between us, but that doesn't mean we should run away from it. You don't strike me as a coward. I personally think we should hang around and see what happens."

She gave a very unladylike snort. "I'm not afraid of anything."

Reaching up, she took his face in her hands and pulled his head down so she could kiss him. Her lips were tentative at first. Testing and teasing him, when her tongue slid between his teeth he was gone. When they finished kissing they were both breathing hard.

Cade willed his body to behave. It wasn't easy when the mere scent of her sent him over the edge. When she touched him, his body was immediately at attention. But that isn't what she said she wanted.

"If you want to take it slower I'm going to need you to stand on the other side of the porch for a minute, because I don't think I can keep my hands off of you," Cade admitted.

She shoved her pelvis against his hardness.

"Patience," he moaned and he wrapped his arms tighter around her.

"I don't want to play it safe," she said as she shoved her hands up his shirt.

Cade's phone rang, but he ignored it.

Then it rang again.

"What?" he answered roughly.

"Is she okay?" Logan asked.

"Yes," he bit out.

"Don't snap at me, GG was worried. She just went to the jail to give Harold a piece of her mind."

Cade smiled. The wrath of his grandmother knew

no bounds and Harold deserved it. "Good," he said as he hung up the phone.

Patience watched him with curiosity in her eyes. "Logan?"

He nodded. "Seems to have an unnatural interest in your well-being."

She smiled. "Are you jealous?"

"Yep."

He kissed her again.

"We better move our party upstairs. My grandmother is on her way home and I don't want her to find us naked on her porch in front of God and everyone."

"Are we about to get naked?" she teased.

"Oh, hell, yeah."

CADE WATCHED AS PATIENCE SLEPT. Her blond hair a halo on her pillow and her lips slightly pink from the kisses they shared. He'd been shocked earlier when she admitted to being jealous. Cade appreciated her honesty and the fact that she was confused by what she felt.

From the little he knew about her past, he could tell that she'd closed herself off from everyone. That she'd given up some of that control to him caused an unnatural need to protect and cherish her.

More than anything he wanted her to understand how much he cared for her.

"Are you going to stare all night or sample the

goods?" Patience's eyes fluttered open and she gave him a lazy grin.

Sliding a hand across her stomach he leaned over and kissed her. "I don't need to sample, I'm ready to buy the whole package."

Patience rolled onto her side threw her leg over his. "I'm not sure how I feel about being a commodity that can be bought and sold."

She nuzzled his neck, her hair smelling of honeysuckle. The scent would forever be burned in his brain as hers.

"You're the one comparing yourself to wares, I'm just telling you I'm buying up the supply. You're my new favorite food, and I plan on tasting every inch of you." He lifted her chin so he could kiss her. He hadn't lied. Patience had become his newest addiction.

Her hand wrapped around his erection. He let out a small grunt of approval.

"I like that plan," she said breathlessly.

Cade gently pulled himself out of her hand and slid down her body. Her perfect breasts were hard peaks and he laved each of them with his tongue until her breath came in short pants. When his hand moved to finger the heat between her legs, her body arched with the contact.

The way she responded to his touch nearly made him explode right then and there. He couldn't believe when he first met her he thought her a prim and proper professor type. If anything she was nothing short of wanton when she was in bed with him, and he would do anything to please her, to hear her moan his name and gasp with delight.

Their bodies truly were made for one another. That was something he couldn't deny. His mouth followed his fingers, and she whispered his name. That was a sound that would never grow old. She needed him, as much as he did her.

Cade nibbled the tiny nub within the folds and she squirmed beneath him. The taste of her was intoxicating. Her hands fisted in his hair and she cried out in release.

He chuckled. "Shh, babe. We don't want to wake up GG."

She didn't seem to hear him. "Cade," she groaned again. This time he covered her mouth with his.

"Inside me," she said. "Please."

She was past that part of reason, consumed by the passion. He wasn't far behind her.

Shifting, he moved her on top of him.

She didn't waste a second before positioning him inside of her and riding him hard. Her hair flew wildly around her head, her breasts moving with the motion. She leaned back shoving herself full on his erection, her nails digging into his thighs. Her eyes were shut as she bounced up and down on him, and he matched her with every thrust.

Her entire body shuddered with release, and Cade pulled her toward him so he could cover the moans he knew were coming with his mouth.

When she collapsed on top of him, he squeezed her tightly. Whatever they had, it was more than he could have ever imagined.

12

THE COMFORTING SMELL OF COFFEE forced Patience to open her eyes. Her disappointment of discovering Cade was already up was quickly quashed when he came through the door with two mugs of coffee and a huge plate of pancakes on a tray.

"Hi," she said as she sat up against the headboard and crossed her legs. He set the tray on the bed and gave her a kiss.

Contented, she sighed against his lips. "Wow. Breakfast in bed?"

"Yes. GG was about to close up the kitchen and I didn't want you to miss out on her chocolate chip pancakes." He positioned the tray on her lap and she inhaled the chocolatey goodness.

"What time is it?" she asked as she reached for her phone.

"Almost ten-thirty."

"Why did you let me sleep so long?"

"Well, we didn't sleep much last night so I thought it wouldn't hurt for you to stay in bed a while longer." He winked at her and she couldn't hide the grin.

After pouring syrup on the pancakes she took a bite. "Mmm. Your grandmother is one amazing cook, that's for sure," Patience said after swallowing a large mouthful of pancake. "So what are you doing today?"

"I'm heading out to the ranch. I was wondering if you might want to come with me."

"That sounds like fun, but I need to follow up with the sheriff this morning. He left me a message late last night on my cell asking if I wanted to press charges against Harold. That man and his cronies are certainly protective of this town. I'm putting them all on my suspect list."

Cade coughed. "Really?"

She shrugged. "Honestly, I don't have anyone else at this point and it gives me a place to start. But before I try to talk to them I need to find out what the dispute was about all those years ago. I have a feeling the records we need are missing for a reason, but I don't know why. And when I do face those ranchers, I want to have my facts straight. That's something I've learned from my friends Katie and Shannon at Stonegate.

"I should also talk to your grandmother some more to see if she knows who might have inside information into the situation that might be willing to talk to me." Patience twisted a couple of curls through her fingers.

"I do have an ulterior motive for inviting you to come out to the ranch with me. Although GG did a good job of keeping the inside of the place fairly clean and up-to-date, I've always sort of ignored my dad's office. I was wondering if maybe we shouldn't check there for some kind of clue."

Patience brightened at the prospect. "You won't mind me rifling through your family's things?"

He shrugged. "Better you than someone I don't know. I thought you could go through his office while I work on the barn door. I promised Deacon, my foreman, I'd get it fixed this weekend so we can store extra hay for the cattle in there."

"That sounds like a plan." She shoveled another forkful of pancake into her mouth.

Cade was staring off into space with a strange look on his face.

She sipped her coffee and the caffeine gave her the jolt her brain needed. "Are you okay?"

He gently tugged a piece of her hair. "Yep, just a busy morning. I'll let you finish your breakfast."

Cade gave her a smile that didn't quite meet his eyes. He stood slowly and left the room.

He was definitely worried about something.

Patience only hoped...

Stop being so damn paranoid.

He's probably thinking about what he has to do

today. Besides, you promised yourself this was a spring fling. Stop taking everything so seriously.

If only her heart would let her.

PATIENCE GASPED WITH DELIGHT and Cade felt an immense sense of pride as they stood in front of the old Victorian. He hadn't lied about the outside being rough. The place needed a new roof, paint, some new windows and the porch was sagging a little in the middle. But those were all cosmetic and the basic bones of the house were strong.

He followed her as she headed up the porch steps.

She cleared her throat. "Uh, I wasn't expecting this." She stepped into the entry.

"Like I told you, it needs work, but it's a great house."

"It's beautiful. It's so comfortable and at the same time stylish." She moved to what was the formal living room. "The furnishings could have been bought yesterday. Everything is so timeless and perfect. Did your mother decorate it?"

At the mention of his mother, Cade sucked in a breath. She'd died when he was twelve, but he still missed her. She'd never been quite the same after his dad disappeared. She always had a quick smile and kind word for him, but the sadness had never left her eyes.

"Yes," he finally croaked out. Everything had been left the way it was when his mother was still alive.

Not a single piece of furniture had been moved. GG never explained why, she only said she was keeping the house for Cade when he decided he was ready to return home. "She and my grandmother were the best at making a house feel like a home. I know how corny that sounds. I loved growing up here. Even during the tough times when my dad wasn't here."

"Your mom made it a safe haven for you, right?" She moved from one room to the next, peeking inside each one.

"Yeah, I guess so." He might not know the real reason behind GG keeping the house the same, but he was grateful. It was like traveling back in time. He could almost hear his mother humming in the kitchen and the sound of his dad talking town business on the phone.

"It's beautiful," Patience said as she turned around in the foyer. The old chandelier was dusty, but still had all the original crystal. That had been a gift from his father to his mother for one of their anniversaries. There was a split staircase going up to the second floor.

"I can't believe these hardwoods are still so perfect and the woodwork on the banisters is amazing. There is real craftsmanship here." She moved her hand along the intricate carvings on the banister.

"Most of what you see is original to the house. It's several generations old. My grandma and my dad were both born here. Dad was the oldest of five brothers and she gave him the house and several thousand acres when he married my mom. My uncles and cousins own the rest of the land. We have about ten thousand acres all together."

"That has to be most of the county." She shook her head. "Well, you're lucky to have such a strong family history. I never knew much about my mother's or father's families, although I sometimes wonder about them."

Since finding out the truth about his father he'd come to acknowledge his ancestors' history a great deal. It no longer hurt him to drive onto the property. Six months ago he'd looked at the place as an investment, but now it was once again home.

"It's a little warm in here," he said. "I can turn the air on, or we can open the windows."

"I'll open the windows. You go ahead and start working on the barn. If I have any trouble, I'll let you know."

There was no mistake. He was being dismissed.

"Patience, I—"

She turned and watched him carefully. "Someone took all this away from you, Cade. I'm going to find a way to give it back. I'm on to something here. I know now that I have to trust my instincts and you have to let me do my job."

"I can help you search in here," he said, pointing to his father's office.

She shook her head. "No. I don't want distractions, and you're a big one. I need to think through the problem. I told you, it needs a methodical approach. You finish what you need to. I'm finding who killed your father."

"DAMN," SHE WHISPERED. She thought about calling Shannon or one of her other friends at SIA, but she didn't want to bring them into her drama.

Opening the top drawer, she fingered through the papers looking for anything of importance. After going through all of the desk drawers, she stood and made her way around the room. The bookshelves were lined with a mixture of popular novels, business books and classics.

The room was painted a coppery color, and with the dark woods it was very much a man's office. For Patience, it gave her context of the man who had lived and worked here. The leather club chairs were comfortable and the art on the walls from talented Texans.

She recognized several pieces, but what surprised her was several framed works of art that were done by tiny hands. There were two stick figures with big smiles standing by a horse with the title "Me and Dad," the artwork was signed by Cade. She gave a tiny gasp. It was obvious that as a child he'd loved his father so much, and then to have lived the way he did thinking his father had abandoned him.

Her hand flew to her chest. She and her brother had done hundreds of pictures for their dad and he treated each one as if it were a Picasso. Cade's father had done the same.

Life with her dad wasn't easy after her brother's disappearance, but he'd always been there for her. Thinking of her dad and brother brought tears to her eyes, but she pushed them away with her fist.

And Cade's poor father, he'd loved his young son. A man didn't hang his child's artwork in expensive frames if he didn't care. The Randall family had missed out on so much because of a terrible tragedy. That was something she had in common with Cade. She understood that pain. The kind not even time could take away.

"Patience?"

She whirled around to find Cade shirtless, his brows drawn in worry. "What's wrong? Did you find something?"

Talking wasn't possible with the giant frog residing in her throat. She shook her head. Her sadness was forgotten at the sight of him with his low-slung jeans resting on his hips. His body was hard and beautiful.

Cade reached her in three steps, his hands on her shoulders.

His concern didn't help. She pushed away from him and walked outside. Leaning her hand on her thighs, she gulped the fresh air. He was right behind her.

"Please, tell me what I can do."

She cleared her throat. "I need some water."

He jogged to the cooler and came back with a bottle, slipping off the cap for her. She sipped it and then blew out a big breath.

Cade watched her carefully. "Tell me what happened."

"It's silly. I promise it isn't worth discussing. Something I saw in your father's office reminded me of my dad and brother. It— I guess it caught me off guard. Our situations aren't so different."

He reached for her and she let him fold her into his arms. His chest was warm and he had the musky smell of a man who'd been working, mixed with his fresh cologne. The intoxicating scents cut through to her baser instincts. She wanted him, more than she'd ever wanted any man.

When he kissed her head, she lifted her face to him.

"I promise I'm fine."

"Can I ask what it was you saw?"

"Your artwork in the beautiful frame. My dad used to do the same thing with the drawings my brother and I did." She lay her head on his chest. "I told you it was silly."

"It isn't silly. I'd forgotten about that. My dad loved Texas artists and craftsmen. This was his dream house and always felt like it deserved the best. He was right and that's why it's so important for me to get the ranch up and running again. I want to honor that memory."

"But you started months ago before you even knew that he'd been killed," she said.

He squeezed her a little tighter. "Yes. One day I realized I'd spent the last ten years running away from this place and this town, but it's home. It always will be. I never plan to live here full-time, but I feel a sense of comfort when I'm here. My mom loved this place as much as my dad, and what you see in there is her stamp on it. Now that I know the truth, well, it's even more important for me to keep what they were trying to do alive."

Extracting herself from his arms, she touched his cheek. "I admire you and what you're doing here. I've done the same sort of thing—running away that is. Only, I haven't had a home in years. Not one like this."

Home for her was a beige condo in a high-rise in downtown Austin. Other than a great view of the Capitol building, there wasn't anything special about it. She even rented the furniture. There were no photos of her family or mementos of her life as a child, though she was certain her father had saved some of those things in boxes. Cade had all of his cousins and GG. Other than texting her dad to let him know she was alive, she had very little contact with him or his new family. She had two stepbrothers and she didn't even know their ages.

The idea of family, of needing to connect with them, made her want to hop on the next plane out of Austin to go and see them.

Finish this case, and then you can go see Pops.

She turned to look at the barn. The two large doors were off and she saw where he'd been sanding the frame. "You work fast."

Taking her hand he led her over to the barn. "You aren't going to believe what I found inside."

Coming in from the sunshine, it took a moment for her eyes to adjust. The barn was huge, much larger than it looked from the outside. Ten horse stalls lined each side of the structure. Some of the doors were falling off, but she could see the possibilities.

To the right was a huge area for hay, but Cade pointed to the left.

"What kind of car is that?"

"A 1967 Shelby GT-500."

"Even I know that's a highly sought after car. You didn't know it was here?"

"Trust me, I'd already have had the baby restored if I knew it was here. I do remember my dad telling me he bought it the day I was born from some guy who was taking it to the junkyard. He said he wanted to spend the next ten years restoring it so I'd have a cool car to drive to school.

"After he—died…" Cade hesitated, the emotion taking over his vocal chords. "Uh—" he coughed "—we closed up the barn. My mom didn't want to mess with the upkeep and I'd totally forgotten about it. It's like finding a treasure chest full of gold. I love cars, and I've always wanted one of these."

She smiled.

"I've called the tow truck to come pick it up and take it to Mr. Lindberg's garage in town. He'll be able to tell me how much work it really needs." His excitement grew the more he talked about the car. She was happy for him, truly so. This car had launched an avalanche of good memories for him. His face filled with joy and he hopped from one foot to the other like a small boy in a candy store.

The crunch of tires on the ground alerted them someone had arrived.

An elderly gentleman met them at the door of the barn.

Cade stuck his hand out to shake the man's hand. "This is my friend Patience. And, Patience, this is the best mechanic in the world, Mr. Lindberg."

The older man tipped his cap. "Nice to meet you, young lady."

She smiled as she shook his hand. He wore gray coveralls that had seen better days, he was slightly stooped and his hair white as cotton.

"I wasn't expecting you to come out," Cade said. "I thought you'd send Deke or one of the boys."

"Cade, I had to see this for myself. Isn't every day you come across a honey of a car like this. Besides we closed early today for the festival." He followed them inside. "Well, would you look at that beauty... I checked the VIN number you gave me, and she's registered. This is a gold mine. Let's check under the hood."

Patience watched them, fascinated by their

adoration for the vehicle. She couldn't help but smile when they whistled their appreciation after checking under the hood.

"I need you to take her to the shop and keep her locked up for me," Cade said. "Had to take the doors off the barn. They're beyond repair, and the new ones don't arrive until Monday."

"Not a problem, son. Can you help me push her out to the drive? I'm not going to be able to lift her in here."

It didn't take them long to get the car loaded onto the back of a trailer. Mr. Lindberg drove off with a big smile on his face.

"Well, that pretty much made my day." Cade slapped a hand against his thigh. "Let me get this other side of the frame sanded and we can go back to town. The festival should be gearing up about now."

"Is there something I can do to help?"

"Would you mind fixing us some lunch? I brought sandwich stuff, and some of GG's fruit salad."

"Not at all. Do you want to eat out here or in the house?"

"Out here is great. The house is still kind of musty."

Patience made the sandwiches while stealing looks under her lashes at Cade. Watching him work was like her own little movie. He was so damn strong and such the opposite of the suit she'd believed him to be when they first met. The rippling muscles in his back made her stomach tighten with need.

"Cade, do you mind if I ask you a few questions about your dad?"

"What do you want to know?" He continued to sand but she noticed the tension lining his eyes.

"If it bothers you, it can wait."

"No, Patience. Just ask the questions."

"You were really young, but do you remember anything about the time right before your father died?"

"Some. Can you be more specific?"

"Were there other people around? I haven't had a chance to talk to any of his friends. Your grandmother told me that most of them have moved away. Then there were those who believed the gossip when he disappeared. But are there certain people you can remember? Or did your dad argue with anyone?"

Cade leaned one arm against the barn. "My uncle Jake was around a lot back then. He was helping my dad out as a foreman during the summers to pay his way through college. They fought all the time but they were brothers and best friends, so I don't think he counts."

Patience didn't want to say it to Cade, but his family members could easily be suspects. The family had seemed so close at the picnic, but she knew better than anyone how easy it was to keep secrets.

"Anyone else?"

"I don't remember who was in it, but there were

ranchers who'd gone in together to buy a large herd of cattle. They pooled their money and split the herd depending on how much they'd contributed. I remember my dad arguing with a few of them but I can't remember why. We were in town one afternoon and my dad and Moses got into it in front of the hardware store. Half the town was watching and I remember sliding down in the seat of our truck because I was embarrassed. But I'm sorry, I can't remember what they were arguing about."

She added Moses to her list that included Harold and Uncle Jake. She'd bet the other men who had harassed her that first day were also part of that group. Funny how those ranchers who had been giving her a hard time kept popping up in her investigation.

"I'm hungry," he said as he shifted away from the barn.

"Me, too," she admitted. But her hunger had nothing to do with food.

13

THE FIREFLY FESTIVAL LIVED UP to its name. The glow from the tiny insects only added to the beauty of the town awash in twinkle lights. As Patience and Cade entered the festival grounds it looked as though a majority of the citizens had turned out along with several hundred tourists.

There were booths with wares, games set up around the park and delicious smells of everything from cotton candy to steak on a stick.

"It's magical," Patience whispered.

"The town goes all out every spring," Cade informed her. He had to admit when he was a kid he'd taken all this for granted. Seeing everything through her eyes made it fresh again. Since their time out at the Triple Dare Ranch she'd been quiet. He didn't know if it was the memories from her past or something else, but he wanted to wash the sadness from her eyes.

Tonight she wore tapered khaki shorts with a lay-ered, white filmy top. Her long blond curls flowed around her giving her an ethereal beauty. She looked like a fairy princess who had lost her wings.

"What would you like to do first? The fair grounds with all the rides are past the food tents. Or we can peruse the booths. Artists from all over come here. If you're hungry we can head over to the tents."

"It doesn't matter to me, but I wouldn't mind look-ing at some of the booths here." She pointed to the right. "Oh, look, it's your friends."

Cade guided her to Andy and Celia's booth. There were four large pieces at the back including a buf-fet and dining table. Nearby he also noted vintage clothing and purses on mannequins and a large case filled with smaller trinkets and jewelry.

"Now that can't be Cade Randall, because if he were in town he would have made a beeline for his favorite girl." Celia stepped from behind the counter to give him a hug. Her belly was almost as big as she was. Always petite, it looked as though she'd swal-lowed three basketballs.

He hugged her as best he could and kissed her cheek. "Guess the rumors are true, Andy got ya knocked up."

Celia smiled as she slapped his shoulder. "Behave. I'm going to be a mom. You have to be more respect-ful. Now who is this beauty? Are you steppin' out on me, Cade?"

"This is my friend, Patience. She's in town helping

to solve my dad's—uh, murder." Those words would always be strange to say.

Celia patted the same shoulder she'd just slapped. "Aw, hon, we always told you he was a good man. GG wouldn't have raised a man who could abandon his family."

She stuck out her hand to Patience. "Andy didn't lie, you are a hot one."

"Celia!" Andy came into the booth holding two steaming cups. "I did not say that."

Handing his wife her drink, he turned to Patience. "I told her that you were beautiful. Beautiful, remember? That's what I said."

Patience laughed. "Speaking of beautiful, is that buffet French? I love the lines." She motioned to one of the larger pieces in the back of the booth.

Celia's smile broadened. "I really do like her," she said as she took Patience's hand and walked her over to the furniture.

"So, what's up with you two?" Andy asked, leaning close to Cade. "You keep watching her like she might run for the hills any minute. Did you have a fight?"

Cade frowned, more frustrated with his lack of understanding than the questioning. "No, we did not have a fight."

"I find flowers and chocolate helpful," Andy interrupted his thoughts. "And when all else fails, jewelry. In fact, I think I have just the thing." He motioned for Cade to follow him over to the glass case.

That's where Cade saw the necklace. Attached to a long silver chain was a delicate fairy holding what looked like the moon in her hands, but the moon was a diamond. The piece was made for Patience.

"That one," Cade murmured. "I'll take it."

Andy shrugged and pulled the necklace from the case. "Do you want me to wrap it up?"

Cade shook his head. "Can you just put some tissue around it or something to protect it while it's in my pocket?"

Andy produced a small sapphire-blue velvet pouch. After taking off the price tag he slipped the necklace into the tiny bag and handed it to Cade. Then Cade gave Andy a handful of bills. "Hey, this is more than we usually make in an entire day at the festival."

"Keep it. With the baby coming you'll have all kinds of expenses."

The other man held his hands up in surrender. "Thanks, Cade."

"What are you two conspiring about now?" Celia asked as the two women walked toward the case.

"I was showing Cade some of the cuff links we have," Andy lied. "He's a Mr. Fancy Pants now and doesn't always wear shirts that button at the cuffs."

Celia stared at her husband. Cade had a feeling his secret would not be safe with Andy for long. Besides, Celia knew everything that was in that case. There was a good chance she'd already noticed the necklace was missing.

"Are you ready to look at some of the other

vendors?" Cade asked Patience. There was a shimmer of tears in her eyes. He glanced at Celia. She mouthed the word "later." Something had transpired between the two women and now Patience was worse than she had been.

Patience had been staring at her toes during the exchange, but she looked up at Cade and said, "Sure." She turned to Celia. "I'm not sure when I'll be back at my place, it depends on the case. Could be a couple of days, could be a week. Can you hold it for me until then?"

"Of course." Celia reached out her arms to hug her. "Let me know and I'll have Andy bring it up on the trailer for you. Now you two go have some fun. There's so much to see now that the festival is bigger than ever."

Cade put his arm around Patience's shoulder and led her away.

"Do you want to go back to GG's? Are you tired?"

"I'm fine." Her voice was hoarse with emotion.

"Patience, please, whatever is making you sad is killing me. Let me help." He turned her so she was facing him.

"I don't know what's wrong with me. I'm a very practical person, but I keep coming across things that remind me of my family. I promised myself I'd shove all this away, but it isn't working.

"My dad sold off all of our furniture when we started traveling full-time. One of the pieces had belonged to my mother and I had always treasured it. It looked exactly like the one in their booth."

"Was it?"

"No. I checked the back of the piece. When he was four, my brother, Jeremy, climbed behind there and drew a life-sized portrait of himself on the wood. My dad thought it was the funniest thing in the world. My mom wasn't too happy at first, but she told me later that it made the piece even more special to her.

"Anyway, it seems like everywhere I turn here there are reminders. I'm beginning to feel like the universe is trying to tell me something. Today at the ranch, well, knowing how much your dad loved you, it made me realize that even though we don't talk as much as we should, my dad really does love me."

Cade didn't like seeing her hurt.

"Do you want to go back to the B and B?"

"No, I'd just be alone with my thoughts there. I'd rather stay busy."

"Well, you wouldn't exactly be alone." Cade waggled his eyebrows at her.

Her laugh came out as more of a snort and her smile lit up her face. "That sounds like a perfectly lovely proposition, but let's hang out here for a little while longer. Besides, I'm not leaving until I get some of that cotton candy you promised and a root beer float and some steak on a stick."

Seeing the woman he met with Deacon last night at the dance, he guided her to the woman's booth.

"Lily?" Cade hoped he remembered her name correctly. "I wanted to bring Patience over to meet you. She's a big fan of Texas artists."

"Oh, it's good to see you again and lovely to meet you, Patience."

The two women shook hands. "The artwork here is beautiful. Did you make it all?" Patience asked.

"I have several paintings here as well as some pottery," Lily said. "My stuff is mixed in with some of the other local artists. Including some of Deacon's woodwork." She pointed out the pieces to Cade.

"I had no idea he did this sort of thing." Cade was surprised by the intricately carved boxes. He was impressed.

Patience asked, "Is there any possibility I could purchase some things and have them shipped to Austin? I don't mind paying the extra charges."

Lily winked at her. "Girl, I'm not going to turn down any kind of sale. I'll drive them personally to your house if I have to."

"I seem to be in a shopping mood tonight, in fact, I'm about to buy way more than my little SUV will hold. Honestly, I don't normally do this sort of thing, but your stuff really appeals to me. I especially like—"

Patience continued talking as the two of them walked toward the pieces. She seemed more animated now, but Cade wasn't sure how much of that was true, and how much was for his benefit.

Cade worried working on his father's case might

be taking too much out of her. She usually worked with the dead and had little contact with the living, who had connections to the remains. This case had hit too close to home for her.

If he had the power he'd fire her, but technically she was consulting for the county. He also had a feeling she wouldn't give up no matter what he said or did. They had to solve this case so they could both move on.

That phrase didn't sit well with him. Move on to where? She'd shared his bed again the night before. This was all new territory for him, too. He wasn't the kind of man who chased women, but this one was worth the effort. Even he was smart enough to figure that one out.

He knew exactly what to do.

14

PATIENCE WOULD NEVER BE A great detective. At least not the kind to chase after suspects and run-down leads.

Her kind of detecting meant using her lab equipment and scholarly mind to reveal what bones could tell her. She'd tested everything from DNA to printer ink over the years, whatever her associates might need. She was part of the machine when it came to solving cases, but here she was it; the investigation of Joseph Randall's demise sat squarely on her shoulders. Should she call in her colleagues to come and help her?

No.

I can do this.

She was a competent scientist and she could solve this as long as she used logic. That had been her problem since she arrived in Phosphor. Never, since the week her brother went missing, had she ever been so emotional. After that, she had had to force herself to stop crying, her father needed her to be the sane and competent one, and that was what she became. From that moment on she refused to let emotions rule her. She didn't go through the teen drama most high school girls did because she focused on her studies. In college she had some one-night stands, but if her date called again she would ignore him. She didn't want to become too attached.

Patience wasn't sure when her guard had slipped. The emotions she'd kept bottled had bubbled to the surface. Unfortunately, she wasn't sure she could control them. Still, there was no way she was giving up now. She'd already learned so much about herself. And there was Cade.

Live beings meant complications; bones had few complications that good science couldn't solve. The human element was messy. And she was definitely a mess. Part of her wished she'd never taken this case on, but that would have meant missing out on meeting Cade. No matter what happened to them in the future, she couldn't deny that being with him was about the best thing that had happened to her in years.

In an effort to move her mind to happier thoughts she searched for the man. Patience had sent him for tea to wash down her corn dog and fried Snickers bar. If she kept eating like this, she would have to buy a new wardrobe soon.

While searching the tent for Cade, she noticed a table of elderly men staring at her. She remembered

Moses, one of the men from the diner. These ranchers were the key to the investigation. She knew it, but she needed proof. Without a witness or some kind of evidence, all she had were rumors and innuendo.

Sitting up a little straighter, she gave them the Patience stare. The one that sent her lab assistants scurrying like frightened mice. The old men quickly turned away and continued their conversation.

She'd talk to the sheriff in the morning and tell him about her suspicions. While she might want to confront these men now, she knew better than to tip them off. No, she would play this one by the book.

Beginning her search again she finally caught sight of him. Logan had stopped Cade with a hand on his shoulder and his cousin was animated as they were talking and laughing.

The exchange pulled her out of her reverie. Moments later, Cade was at her side, handing her a cup of tea. "I saw you chatting with your cousin. What was so funny?"

"Things around here can sometimes get to be like a real-life soap opera. Charli likes Hemi, who is dancing with Michele. But Charli's too much of a chicken to ask him to dance. Logan and I were daring her to do it."

Patience frowned.

"What is it?" he asked.

"Well, I spend a lot of time in my office. My friends there often have drama in their lives, but I don't get to see a lot of it in person. The anthropologist in me is fascinated, but I'm never happy knowing my friends are struggling or—"

"Love is messy," Cade said, as he squeezed her hand.

"I was thinking the same thing. Life is messy in general. I have a tendency to live in a very sterile environment."

He watched her carefully.

"Before—I wanted to tell you that I'm not normally so emotional. In fact, before I arrived in Phosphor, the last time I cried was when I received my first doctorate five years ago."

"Five? That would have made you twenty-one." He put an arm around her shoulder. "What was it about it that made you cry?"

"It's dumb really. My dad had promised to come to see me walk the stage. I hadn't seen him in two years, and he didn't make it. He was caught up in a dig in Turkey. I don't know why, but in that moment I felt more alone than I ever had." She twisted away from Cade's arm. "I seem to spill my guts whenever you're around. Pretty soon, you're going to know my whole life story, which isn't very exciting."

"Patience, I want to know everything about you. I'm interested in you."

She sighed. "Thanks. You're sweet. I'm not normally such a drama queen. An ice queen, maybe."

Cade chuckled. "I have a hard time believing that. You're the hottest woman I've ever met. I'm drawn to you like a bug to a flame."

How did he always know the right thing to say?

"When I first met you, I would have never imagined you being so charming," she said honestly.

He chuckled again. "That was the day from hell for me. I'd invested a ton of time in a merger and taken a huge risk. The deal was going to take my company and the one we were merging with to the next level and it has. When the sheriff called and asked me to meet him at your office, I honestly considered skipping it.

"So when you mentioned my dad, well, all those defenses went up immediately. Then I was in shock. I don't even remember walking back to the car that was waiting for me. I don't remember the meetings where we signed the final contracts, or the celebration afterward. It was like I'd stepped into some strange movie and I couldn't get out."

She lay her head on his shoulder. "I realize now how much information you had to process. Finding out after all those years that your father didn't abandon you. The sheriff kept telling me you were a great guy. Although I had a hard time believing him that day, he was right."

Kissing the top of her head he squeezed her to him. "At least I have closure. I wish I could help you find the same."

She sighed deeply. "Yeah, I've been thinking about that, too. You were right about using my resources. When we finish this case, I'm going to get my friends at Stonegate to help me."

"Good for you."

"Yea, me," she joked. "Before, I figured that if I never knew the real truth, a part of me could stay hopeful, but after everything that has happened the last few days, well, it won't be easy. The case is more than thirteen years old, but if anyone can crack it, my colleagues can." Her voice caught. "We were so close, Jeremy and me. When my mom died, well, he became my touchstone. If he is alive…I'll be the happiest woman ever."

Patience decided she'd been depressed long enough. Just talking about everything lightened her heart.

"We need to get some exercise," she said as she stood. "After that fried Snickers bar, my butt is getting bigger as I speak."

Cade laughed. "I happen to be very fond of your butt," he said, sliding his hand seductively down her back. "I have an idea of a really great exercise we can do, but we need some privacy."

Patience smiled. "We'll do that workout later, I was thinking I'd like to dance. This band is really good."

"Okay, but with one condition."

"What?" She looked up through her lashes at him.

"I'm not sharing you with anyone tonight. All the dances are mine. You're mine."

Those words sent heat coursing through her body. She was ready to drag him back to the B and B. "I'm good with that," she said against his lips before he kissed her. They stayed that way for almost a minute before someone whistled.

They reluctantly pulled apart and Cade led her to the floor.

She was his in more ways than he would ever know.

15

TWO HOURS LATER, they were heading back to the B and B. Cade wanted to throw her over his shoulder and run with her. He wasn't sure how much longer he could go without making love to her.

Tonight he wanted them both to be free to be as wild as they wanted. Not that either had held back before.

"I want to take you somewhere special tonight, Patience. It's a surprise."

"Cade, I'll go wherever you want to take me." She squeezed his hand.

They sprinted for the truck and he fished out his keys. "Get in, we have to stop at the B and B and get a couple of things. It'll only take two minutes." He kissed her hard and then they took off.

Soon, he'd stashed a duffel bag and a cooler in the truck and they were on their way.

"Now I'm really curious. Where are we going?"

"I promise you'll like it." Cade turned up the music in the truck. Tonight it was important for her to see that this was more than a casual fling for him. The words might be difficult to say, but he could show her.

He turned onto his property.

"Are we at your house?" She sounded surprised.

Cade grinned. "Not exactly."

She chuckled. "Way to be vague."

Instead of going up to the house he turned to the right on a small side road.

The trees opened up to a pond. The full moon was the only light along with a million stars. It was exactly the setting he wanted.

"This lake is on your property?" she asked as he helped her out of the truck.

"It's too small to be a lake, but it's a pretty large pond."

She turned her head as if listening for something. "Is there a waterfall?"

Cade motioned for her to follow him over some rocks.

A minute later they were at the falls. The rocks under the falls jutted out in all different directions and a strange greenish glow lit the rocks and the water.

A gasp came from Patience as she noticed the glow. "This is beautiful, why does the water do that?"

"When I was a kid, my mom and dad told me it

was fairy magic, and I believed them. Later I found out it's from the algae in the soil around the rocks. It's not so high an amount that it's dangerous to humans, but it's enough that it makes the water glow at certain times of the year."

"I'm a scientist and I like the fairy explanation better," she told him.

"We can leave our clothes here on this rock," he said, stripping off his shirt.

"What?"

He turned to find her staring at him with an incredulous look on her face.

"I want to take you skinny-dipping. You know, where you get naked in the water? It's what we do in the country." Cade reached for the hem of her blouse and pulled it over her head.

"I know what skinny-dipping is, but someone might come by." She stopped his hands from unbuttoning the top of her shorts. "This has to be a popular place, even if it is private property, especially for kids who want to make out."

Cade continued his work on her shorts sliding them down her long legs. A vision in her pink bra and panties, he wanted to take her right then. His libido was in full throttle.

"It's pretty far from town and kind of remote." He unhooked her bra and her nipples tightened into peaks with the soft breeze. Cade couldn't wait to taste her, but he slid down the panties. Forcing himself away from her, he pulled off his boots, socks and jeans.

"You mean to tell me you never brought a girl out here to skinny-dip before?" She followed him under the falls.

He led her to a pool where the hot spring fed water from underneath and mixed with the cool water, which made the temperature perfect no matter what time of year it was.

Cade stepped into waist deep water and reached for her. "You are the first girl I've ever brought here. GG always thought it best if we didn't tell anyone about this place. She didn't want someone, especially kids, getting hurt out here."

"But you brought Andy?"

"Yep. But he took a blood oath, we both did. We became the Secret Keepers of the Brotherhood."

Her throaty laugh warmed him to the core. "That sounds serious. Now I believe I can trust you with all of my secrets."

He gave her a chivalrous bow before helping her into the pool. "Milady, the Brotherhood is known for our discretion. We consider ourselves professional secret keepers."

Patience gave him a sweet smile.

"Am I really the only woman you've brought here?"

"Yes." He nipped her ear. Cade pulled her with him as moved backward onto a small slab carved out of the rock. There were several in the pool that made excellent seats.

"I feel so special," she said as she turned and sat on his lap.

"You are special." He kissed her neck. They both stared out at the water sluicing down the rocks above them for a minute. He wanted to tell her how much she meant to him, but the words just wouldn't come out.

"With the sounds of the water and crickets, I could go to sleep here."

"That's not really what I had in mind." One of his hands slid across her belly and down to the folds of pink flesh below.

Patience gasped his name as she squirmed on his lap. If he never heard another sound in his life, that sound of pleasure would be enough for him.

"Babe, you are the most incredible creature I've ever met in my life." He nibbled her ear. "The glow from the water makes you look like a wanton fairy princess."

Her butt slid up and down his erection as she rocked against his fingers. It was all he could do to keep himself under control.

Patience had begun to pant and he could feel the tension in her body. Increasing the pressure on the nub he moved his fingers faster until she moaned her release as her body collapsed against him.

"Oh, I'm not done with you yet." Cade picked her up and sat her on the rock bench while he grabbed one of the foil packets from his jeans. He'd brought several just in case. He put the sheath on his cock before sliding back into the water.

Patience had a strange look on her face.

He touched her cheek with his hand. "What are you thinking about?" Sitting down, he pulled her back onto his lap, facing him this time.

"You." She held his face in her hands. "I met you a few days ago and I feel like a different person. In a good way." She kissed him as she positioned herself on top of him.

"I already thought you were perfect," he said.

"Pfhhwut. Not hardly."

Cade slid his hands down her sides and over her beautiful butt. "Oh, yes. I'm very hard."

He nuzzled her neck and kissed her.

She sighed lazily. "I can't think when you do that."

"Thinking is highly overrated." He kissed her again, delighted by her admission.

Her hand went to his shoulder. Lifting her body she rode him hard and fast. When she leaned back with her hands on his thighs and her breasts in the air, he nearly lost control. Gritting his teeth he held on.

A second before he thought he couldn't take any more of the ecstasy, her muscles contracted and her body shuddered. Cade spilled himself into her as he held her close to his chest.

Face flushed and eyes hazy with satisfaction, she

really was the most gorgeous creature he'd ever met. And she was his—at least for now.

IT WAS ALMOST FOUR IN THE morning before Patience and Cade tiptoed into the B and B. They fell into his bed, exhausted from making love in the pool and under the stars in the back of his truck.

Patience snuggled into Cade. No one had ever made her feel as safe and secure as he did. For the first time she could see why someone would allow themselves to depend on another person for comfort. Why people were often truly committed to long-term relationships.

Cade's arm tightened around her waist and she sighed with contentment. The man did things to her. Every time their bodies connected she lost a little bit more of herself to him. Tonight had been the loveliest, most romantic one of her life.

The way he looked at her when they made love, assured her he felt as deeply as she did. Tonight it was almost as if he had to show her they were meant for one another. When he'd whispered "mine" after their escapade in the pool, a delightful shiver had spread through her body. That tiny bit of possessiveness made her feel powerful.

She also liked what she could do to his body, and if she were honest, she thought of him as hers. The idea of anyone else touching him—well, she now understood why women fought over men. Cade would be worth it.

Still, it scared her that everything seemed to be moving so fast, and she had no experience with this type of relationship. Cade made it seem easy. Still, he might have feelings for her now, but how long would they last? From her friends she'd learned that often the hotter the passion in the beginning the faster it burned out.

Her eyes flashed open. The case. She'd spent so much time with Cade that she'd completely lost her focus. That was something that had never happened before.

Her instincts told her she should return to the murder site. The ring she found was several feet from the bones and shallow grave. It could have come off during a struggle and the killer hadn't seen it. That was one logical explanation because it would have been smarter for Joseph's killer to bury everything with him in the sandy soil. The ring was covered with years of dirt and grime and she doubted the lab would pick up any prints.

Still, she felt as if there was more. If there was a struggle where the ring had been and not where the bones were, well, she needed to do a more thorough search.

Pausing for a moment, she listened to Cade's soft snores. Gently removing his arm, she stuffed a pillow under it. After making a stop in the bathroom to brush her teeth and hair, she slipped on a clean shirt and pair of jeans and her boots. The run-in with the snake the other day taught her to protect her feet and legs.

Grabbing her keys and purse, she headed down the hallway. She was at the stairs before she realized she should probably leave a note for Cade, but she didn't want to risk waking him up. She needed time to work without distraction, and she wanted time to think.

Physical evidence of a struggle would give her something solid to take to the sheriff. She could give him the list of suspects and they might very well be on to solving the case.

But what happened once the case was solved? Would the bond she and Cade had formed during the past few days last beyond the county lines? Never in her life had she wanted a human being like she did Cade.

You keep telling yourself that.

The problem was the idea of saying goodbye to Cade didn't sit well with her.

"And it's absolutely frightening how much he makes me feel," she muttered, turning the key and starting the engine.

16

FOR MORE THAN AN HOUR, Patience studied the area near the tree line, which was about forty feet from where Joseph Randall had been buried. The fragments of bones around the chest area indicated he had been shot at close range, almost as if the barrel of the rifle had been against his chest.

What if he'd been fighting with someone and the gun had gone off? Patience wrote her thoughts down in the notebook she carried.

The who and the why of the argument weren't quite as important as the how at this stage of her investigation. She retraced her steps around the area where she'd run into the snake. There had been a small patch of dirt perfect for her car behind the cluster of trees where she didn't have to worry about not having four-wheel drive.

Finding a large stick, she shook some of the low growth around the trees before stepping up to them.

She didn't want to surprise any more reptiles or small creatures that might have burrowed into the earth.

The third tree in the long row caught her attention. The tree had grown over the past twenty years, but about a foot above her head was a five-by-two-inch gash. The mark could have been made by any number of things. Though the edges had worn away with the elements, the shape was distinctive.

The butt of a rifle, which meant the killer had been backed into the tree while holding the gun. Reaching up on her tiptoes she scraped some of the bark into an evidence bag. There was little hope of finding anything after all these years, but she'd been in the business a long time and stranger things had happened.

She'd knelt down to close up the bag and put it in the case she brought. The rifle butt on the tree told her there was a possibility that this was where Joseph had been killed and his body moved to the grave site.

The sheriff's deputy hadn't known to leave the body where it was until she could get there. The coroner had brought the bones to Austin and that was where she discovered the victim had been shot at close range with a rifle. When she arrived the other day she suspected the man had been killed one place and moved to the spot under the oak tree.

The gash in the tree confirmed her suspicions. Bending down she used a small scoop to gather soil samples from around the area. There was a good chance her lab assistants would find nothing, but she had to be thorough. Blood and DNA samples had a way of showing up in the oddest places. She was good at her job because she never assumed anything. She collected the data and would let the science do its job.

Standing up, she stared at the gash again. The angle looked as though the shooter held the gun and was backed into the tree. Had the shooter been shoved and the gun went off?

Patience chewed on her lip for a second. That would explain the odd angle of the shot. Scraping some more samples from around the gash she filled three more evidence bags. It was a long shot but there was a chance the hair from the shooter or DNA might still be in the bark of the tree.

Her work was her solace and today it didn't disappoint.

More than an hour later she put away her case and tossed her gloves in the small receptacle she had in the back of her car. Hot and grimy, a shower was next on her list of things to do. Then she would have to pack up and head back to her lab. The idea of leaving Cade tugged at her gut, but it was time to slow things down. She had work to do. She also didn't want the complication of anything like a long-term relationship.

Liar.

No. She had to do what was best for her sanity

and making a clean break was the right course of action.

You're tied up in him, and it's going to break your heart.

At first there might be some temporary sadness, but the feelings weren't as deep as she thought. She would get over him soon. At least that's what Patience told herself as she shut the trunk.

The sound of a truck barreling down the road caught her attention.

Thinking it might be Cade, she started to step out through the trees when she saw the truck was an older model and a different color.

Why would anyone be out here at this time of day? It's not even six in the morning.

The truck door slammed, and she stayed behind the cover of the trees, which also hid her vehicle.

When Harold, the cranky rancher, came around the hood of his truck she was glad she'd stayed where she was. The last thing she needed was to meet that guy when she had no more protection than a big stick.

For several minutes Harold stared down at the ground of the shallow grave. A tear slid along the man's cheek, and he bent over with his hands on his thighs as if he was trying to catch his breath.

"Damn you, Joe. Damn you." Harold straightened and kicked the dirt around the grave. "If you hadn't pushed me that night. Haven't had a moment's peace in twenty years and it's all your fault. I didn't know the damn thing was loaded. I came out here to make you see reason. Never meant to hurt you. You—ruined everything." His voice was rough with tears.

She had her killer.

Whatever had happened, Patience's gut told her it likely hadn't been planned. The man's face was tortured with grief, and when he sniffled and ran a hand over his eyes to wipe away the tears, she almost felt sorry for him.

Except this was the guy who had robbed Cade of his father and nearly destroyed his family. Cade had said his mother was never the same after his dad had died.

Harold kicked at the dirt again and then stared out at the rising sun.

Something rustled near her feet and she glanced down to see a large copperhead slithering across her boots. This time Patience didn't dare move or make a sound. One, she didn't want to alarm the snake and have it strike out at her. Two, she also didn't want to jump through the bushes and have Harold notice her. If he did, well, he wouldn't be happy about what she had just heard and witnessed.

She took short shallow breaths while she stared down at the creature.

Harold's truck roared to life and she glanced up in time to see two rifles attached to a rack in the rear of his truck.

She had her killer and possibly even the weapon. Unfortunately, she had no hard evidence. The sheriff could get a judge to give him a warrant for the weapon, but only if she had more than a suspicion. She remembered Shannon's advice about building her case, and that's what she had to do.

Which took her back to square one. Well, not really. She knew Harold was her killer, but now she needed physical evidence. If the butt of the gun had scratches on it consistent with what she found on the tree, that would help but it was a long shot. A triangle formed in her mind. The ranchers, the water rights and Joseph. Cade had said something about them buying a bunch of cattle together and separating the herd. What if they'd also agreed to share water rights? She was brainstorming, but it fit. She wasn't exactly sure how water rights worked. Shannon had explained that, legally, it was a cobra's nest of property and river or lake rights. It depended if the water flowed from public water like lakes or rivers, or from underground wells.

While she might understand the logistics, her gut once again told her that this was all somehow related. Maybe Harold and some of the other ranchers felt Joseph was trying to cheat them in some way. Then there's Cade's uncle and the arguments they'd had just before Joseph died. Surely that was just a coincidence?

Her gut twisted into a tight knot. What if Harold wasn't the only killer? All those ranchers had been giving her mean looks. Was it possible that Uncle

Jake was covering for them? No. He didn't seem like that kind of man.

But how much do you really know about him? Or any of the ranchers, for that matter?

Patience stood there for another few seconds waiting for the snake to move, and finally it slithered on. Breathing deep, she gathered her things. Taking a picture of the gash in the tree with her digital camera, she stored it in her pocket. She needed to see the sheriff right away and tell him about her suspicions. Loading up her car, she sped toward town.

It was up to her to prove if she could see this case through.

CADE WAS DISAPPOINTED Patience wasn't in his bed when he woke up. The last thing he remembered was her naked body tucked next to his and everything feeling right with the world.

He didn't hear the shower running, so he figured she'd gone down for some coffee or breakfast. Glancing at the clock he saw it was only seven, part of him wanted to go back to sleep, but he had a lot to do out at the ranch. He hoped Patience would be able to join him while she carried on the investigation.

After showering and changing clothes, Cade went in search of the woman who consumed his thoughts these days.

Downstairs he was surprised when she wasn't in the dining room. He pushed through the kitchen door to see if she was talking with GG. His grandmother was alone.

He kissed her on the cheek and grabbed one of the cinnamon rolls from the platter she had on the counter. Taking a large bite he moaned. "I tell you if you mass-marketed these things, you'd make a billion dollars," he said.

"They only taste so good because they came from my oven. No one makes 'em like I do."

"True. You haven't seen Patience around have you? I knocked on her door and she didn't answer this morning."

His grandmother chuckled. "Knocked on her door? Listen, she's a smart girl with a good head on her shoulders, and she's kindhearted. There's also something sad inside her, gnaws at my gut that someone so sweet has suffered such sorrow. Don't suppose you'd know what that is?"

Cade frowned. "I have an idea, but it's not my story to tell. You'll have to ask her."

GG eyed him carefully. "She doesn't look it but she's fragile," she said. "Don't treat her like some weekend fling."

So, they really hadn't been as sneaky as they thought. Cade could feel the heat on his cheeks. No one but his grandmother could make him blush.

"I know she's special. I promise I do. In fact—" Cade stopped himself.

"Tell me."

"I—" To find the right words was difficult. "I care

about her. More than anyone I've ever met. There, are you happy?"

She gave him the GG eye, where she summed an entire thought up in one glance. "Like I said, you treat her right. And if I hear otherwise, there will be hell to pay."

"Yes, ma'am. Do you know where she is? Did she go for a walk?"

"Nope. I put the first batch of rolls in around five this morning and her car was gone. Wherever she went, she left awful early."

Her car was gone? Cade felt a moment of panic. Stuffing the rest of the roll in his mouth, he waved goodbye to his grandmother and ran back up the stairs two at a time.

The only thing that kept him sane was that her clothes and toiletries were still in her room. He had worried that last night had been too much and he'd maybe scared her off. When they made love he felt as if he'd laid bare his soul to her.

But she'd stayed by him until…he was asleep.

Then she left.

Cade grabbed his keys and wallet.

Calm down. She's probably taking a drive or maybe she went to the diner.

At four in the morning?

Climbing into his truck, he forced himself to take a deep breath. Why the hell was he freaking out? She probably left to take care of something with the case.

He put the truck in Drive and headed out to the site where his father had been killed.

There were tire tracks, but they'd come from a truck, not her little car.

Something caught his eye in the grove of trees to the left. As he moved closer he saw it was her red bandana she used to wipe the sweat off her forehead. He stepped through the underbrush and between the trees. She had been there. Her tire tracks were still fresh. He squeezed the bandana in his hands. Where was she now?

He drove immediately to the sheriff's office, but didn't see her car. He decided to circle by the diner in case she'd gotten hungry. That's when he spotted her car parked in front of the courthouse.

He tried the courthouse door, but it was locked. Glancing around the square there wasn't much open except the diner and he checked to make sure she wasn't in there.

Had she been kidnapped?

He ran back to the sheriff's office. "Sheriff, have you seen Patience?"

"Sure. She's at the courthouse. Let her in a little while ago. Says she doesn't want to be disturbed. Why?"

"I was worried about her."

"You didn't try calling her?'"

The phone. Cade felt like an ass. He had her cell number, why hadn't he just called Patience? Instead, he'd run off like a crazy fool.

Where the hell is my head?

You're in love with a beautiful woman and you can't think straight.

Love? Oh, hell. It just might be.

Pulling his phone from his pocket, he searched for her contact listing.

"She's supposed to call me when she wants to leave," the sheriff said.

"Give me your keys, please?"

"Son, she said she didn't want anyone bothering her."

"I'm not just anyone. Besides, if she doesn't want me there, I promise I'll leave."

The sheriff watched him for a full thirty seconds. "All right, but don't be pestering. She's doing your family a huge favor and you need to let her do her job."

"Promise," he said and he meant it. He only needed to see her and make sure she was okay. That was all.

Beau handed over the keys.

Cade walked back to the courthouse, unlocked the door and then locked it again behind him.

At the bottom of the basement stairs he watched as Patience went through every file in a box. She hadn't noticed him because she was so involved with her work.

"Hey," he said, "and I've been looking all over town for you. Where have you been?"

She turned around quickly and gave him a hard

stare. For some reason she didn't seem so happy to see him. "I've been working on the case. I asked that I not be disturbed."

Her vagueness and the sharp tone surprised him.

"Is something wrong?"

After a moment she said, "I really need to work." She turned back to her files.

If she'd slapped him it wouldn't have hurt any less.

What is going on?

"Can I help?"

She shook her head. "I prefer to work alone."

"Fine, but tell me what's upset you. Why are you mad at me?"

She glanced up at him then. "I'm not mad. I'm busy. I should have been doing more from the beginning, I've spent most of my time—"

With me.

"What I'm doing right now is an important part of solving your father's murder and I need to focus."

"Okay, so you think I'm a distraction. But I don't have to be. Let me help you." It almost sounded like begging, and Cade wanted to kick himself for it. Since when did he beg a woman for anything?

Oh, shut it. Last night you would have been her willing slave for one more taste of her.

But this wasn't his passionate lover. This was the same woman he'd met in her office six days ago, businesslike and straight to the point. The loving woman who drove him to the edge of sanity every time they made love was gone.

She sighed. "Look, I don't mean to be rude. I'm tired. I didn't get much sleep, and I'm not going to until I find those records we were searching for the other day."

Cade noticed the white around her mouth and her normally rosy cheeks were pale. She was stressed.

"Why don't I search, while you go back to the B and B and get some sleep? I don't understand the sudden rush."

She hesitated, as if she wanted to tell him something important, but then changed her mind. "You don't know me well enough to understand my OCD tendencies. I have to search every piece of evidence myself and know that a thorough job has been done. Please, Cade. The faster you leave, the faster I can get through this."

"Sure." There was no use in arguing with the stubborn woman. She didn't want him here. "I'll leave you to your work."

He stomped up the stairs never feeling more useless than he did in that moment.

_17_

"THAT COULD HAVE GONE BETTER," Patience admonished herself. Poor Cade. All he'd wanted to do was help, and she'd turned him away like an errant child. The hurt in those beautiful eyes of his made her heart ache.

When he appeared she'd seen the relief on his face. She should have left him a note.

Her brain had started the process of putting the pieces together and so many scenarios ran through her head that the last thing she needed was Cade front and center.

There was also the fact the sheriff had told her not to share her suspicions with the Randall family until they had some hard proof.

Keeping the truth from Cade wasn't easy for her. She was an honest person, but this was a necessity. The only way she could think to keep him away was being rude.

Being my normal self.

It had worked, perhaps too well.

She hadn't lied about needing to peruse every single file on her own. It was the only way her brain could be certain she hadn't missed anything. In the last two hours she'd made some good progress, only ten more boxes to go.

After brainstorming with the sheriff, they'd decided the missing water files had something to do with the night Joseph was killed. Harold and Joseph had been out in the middle of nowhere, and the river ran not two hundred feet from where the grave had been. Did Harold need those water rights for his property, which bordered the east side of the burial spot?

"From the way he's been acting toward you and what you saw out at the site, it seems Harold could be our man." The sheriff agreed with her. "You keep searching for those files. Now that we have this new lead I'll start digging around a few other places. Let me know if you find anything else."

As she opened the last box she prayed the files would be in there. They weren't.

Dejection filled her. There was a good chance Harold had stolen the files, and without a motive it would be difficult to prove their case, even if she found his DNA at the site. Short of a full confession, there wouldn't be anything they could take to trial.

Frustrated, she put everything back where she found it. Yawning, she pulled up in front of the

B and B. Having been up so early that morning she was finally feeling the effects. She definitely needed her bed.

There was hammering on the roof.

She glanced up to see Cade watching her. With his shirt off and the sun behind his back, he looked like a Roman god. She waved up to him, but he didn't smile.

I probably deserved that.

She could feel his gaze on her as she walked toward the porch. A raw ache filled her stomach, and hammering or no, she knew she had to get some rest.

That was just as well. Separating herself from Cade would be difficult and it might help things along if he were angry with her.

Slipping between the sheets, she listened to the dull thud on the roof. At least he was there. He might not ever talk to her again, but she'd still see him.

Her eyes drooped, and she snuggled into the pillow, wishing more than anything his comforting arms were around her.

CADE WATCHED HER SLEEP from the doorway. She must have been exhausted. Maybe that explained why she'd been so cross with him earlier. Well, part of it, anyway. There had been something she wanted to tell him, but she hadn't trusted him enough.

His temper had cooled and he knew that now. During the early morning she'd realized something about the case. She'd gone out to the burial site, and then to the sheriff since he'd been the one to let her in.

Cade wasn't such an idiot that he couldn't put the pieces together. It hurt that she didn't trust him—especially after everything they shared the past few days. But he'd come to know her well, and if she was hiding something from him, it was because she wanted to protect him.

There was no other answer.

Pushing people away was what she'd done all of her life. She'd admitted it more than once. Those walls she'd had when they first met had gone back up. He remembered what she said about being called the ice queen.

Whoever gave her that label was an imbecile.

The woman was as hot as they came and she made love as passionately with her whole heart. He'd never been with a woman who gave herself so completely.

So she was a little cranky when she was tired, who wasn't?

She stretched and he sucked in a breath as her breasts pushed against the taut T-shirt.

"Cade?" She blinked as if she were looking at an apparition.

"I was just checking to see if you want some lunch. GG sent me up."

Liar.

Yes, but it's for a good cause.

"What time is it?"

"Almost two."

She sat straight up and slipped off the side of the bed.

Cade's jeans felt tight in the crotch area. God forgive him.

"I didn't mean to sleep so long. I'm afraid I'll have to skip lunch, but tell GG I said thanks."

Her tone was kinder this time, but she was giving him the brush-off again.

"How about I have her pack it up so you can take it with you?" He said it casually, but more than anything he wanted to know what was so important.

Shoving the hair from her eyes she gazed up at him. "I'm sorry about before. Once I—well, I tend to be single-minded when I'm working."

"I'm the same way. Remember the first day we met? You'd given me news that should have had me on the floor, but I had to deal with my biggest problem first, which was taking care of my employees."

She wrung her hands as if she were anxious. "Look, I'm onto something, but I don't feel like sharing my theory quite yet. One, I might look like an idiot if I'm wrong, and two, well, I like to have my facts straight before any accusations are made."

Cade cleared his throat. "I understand that. I'm sorry I was so pushy before. I guess we were both tired."

"I didn't like fighting with you." She pursed her lips.

"Yep. Me, either." More than anything he wanted to kiss her.

"I can't let emotion get in the way of this case."

"Are you saying we're finished?"

She nodded. "For now. That may sound cruel, but your father deserves my undivided attention. I have to get to my lab and examine the evidence I found this morning."

"So you're going back to Austin now?"

Her hands were on her hips. "I have to. Don't you want me to solve your father's murder?"

Of course he did.

Patience grabbed her small suitcase from the closet and carefully folded her clothes into it.

What could he say to stop her? Should he say anything? Was it better this way? He was as confused as she likely was. Maybe time would help them both.

Before he could get any words out, she paused, holding a small print she'd bought the night before at the fair. It was a small depiction of the town square.

"What is it?"

After placing the art in her suitcase. She stared down at her toes. "It has to be there." She glanced up at him. "Can you take me back out to your place? I need to check your dad's office."

"Sure, but I thought you went through it yesterday."

"I did." She pinched the bridge of her nose with

her thumb and finger. "I missed something. I know I did."

Cade wondered what was so important, but kept his mouth shut. She needed him to take her out to his ranch, and for that he was grateful. He wouldn't push her again until she was ready to share. Whatever it was she saw in the painting, it haunted her.

PATIENCE WAS LOST IN HER reverie. She'd been staring out the window of Cade's father's office for several minutes thinking about how she felt earlier at the B and B when she woke up from her nap and found him watching her. At first she thought she'd been dreaming.

He had been watching her with such concern. Patience kept her distance and tried to make him understand why she had to leave.

He'd been respectful. He even met her halfway when it came to his father's case. On the drive out he hadn't asked her a single question. She knew it was killing him, but the fact that he didn't push made her admire him even more.

He and his foreman pounded away on the barn doors and she tried to clear her head. This was no time to think about Cade. Something she'd seen in that painting had triggered her brain, telling her to go back to the family homestead. Something was there.

She stood and made her way slowly around the room, scrutinizing every piece of art, furniture and even the floor as she went. Making her way around the desk she focused on the four framed pictures of Cade's childhood artwork. Something about the crude drawings had dredged up emotions she'd been pushing down for years.

"There's something here," she whispered.

Lifting one of the pieces off the wall, she saw exactly what she hoped for—the corner of a safe. She quickly took down the other pictures. It had been there all along. She pulled on the handle but it was locked. Her gut churned. Every instinct she had pointed to that safe.

Racing outside, she found Cade and the foreman talking in the barn.

"Cade?"

"Are you okay?" He walked over to her and put his hands on her shoulders. "You're flush."

"I ran. I need your help with something."

She smiled at Deacon.

The man dipped his hat. "I'm headed out to check the cattle, anyway." He waved them off.

"What's up?" Cade followed her into the house.

Leading him into his father's office, she motioned toward the safe.

By the shock in his eyes and the crinkling of his forehead she knew he'd had no idea the safe was there.

"It's locked. Do you know the combination?"

He shrugged. "I've never seen it before."

"Chances are the combination is something simple."

"How did you know it was there?"

She stood next to the safe. "My dad always said my artwork and my brother's were his most precious treasures. That meant a lot to us since he had a huge art collection, which filled our house. I just had a feeling that your dad felt the same way. We should try to open it." Pursing her lips, she tapped a finger against them. "What was your mother's birth date?"

Cade rattled off the numbers but they didn't work.

"Tell me your birthday."

He sat on the edge of the desk and called out the numbers. This time there was a click.

"It can't be that easy." She pulled on the handle and it opened. Inside were a number of folders and a carved wooden box. She handed the box to Cade and set the files on the desk.

Some of the files contained birth certificates, passports and that sort of thing. Then she found other things that made her heart thump loudly. The first was a date book. She thumbed through to the day Joseph had disappeared. Harold's name was the only item scribbled on that page. Her breath caught. Then she pulled out a number of papers in the back of the book. There were several contracts. As she read them, she began to understand. There were four lease agreements with four different ranchers. The first two names she recognized, Harold and Moses. She bet the sheriff would know the rest if the men were still in Phosphor.

Closing her eyes she took a deep breath. This might be enough, at least for the sheriff to bring Harold in for questioning. It was still circumstantial, but if the sheriff could confiscate Harold's gun, she could have the lab do the ballistics check. The lease agreements weren't signed, which meant something had held up the process. If the sheriff didn't know, her friend Chi at Stonegate, their resident lawyer, might be able to figure it out.

She'd done it. Excitement bubbled to the surface and she almost squealed.

There was a choking sound behind her.

Turning, she saw Cade with a tortured look on his face.

What had been in that box?

18

THE KNOT OF PAIN IN HIS CHEST tightened as Cade examined the items in the box. His baby shoes, the first tooth he lost and pictures of the first time he rode a horse were only a few of the items included from his childhood. Cade fingered his grade one report card and several letters he'd written to his dad when his father had to travel for business.

"Cade?"

Patience's worried eyes took in his face and she touched his cheek.

He set the box on the desk so she could see it.

"Oh," she whispered.

Picking up the baby shoes gingerly she glanced up at him. "He loved you so much." Her voice hoarse with emotion. "These really must have been his most precious treasures. I don't know anyone who keeps baby shoes in a safe."

The air in the house was stifling. He had to get

out, almost running for the door. Bellowing at the sky seemed appropriate as he kicked through the dirt on the way to the barn. But he wouldn't embarrass himself that way. Before he even knew what he was doing, he picked up a bale of hay his foreman had brought and stacked it in the area they'd cleaned out. By the twentieth bale, his muscles were screaming and sweat dripped from every pore, but he kept on.

For so long he'd hated a man who had obviously loved him more than anything. Patience was right. No one kept baby stuff in a safe.

Cade sat down on one of the hay bales and put his head in his hands.

Would his father ever forgive him for thinking the worst? Cade had betrayed the man's memories by turning him into a monster. When in truth, his father had never been anything but kind to him.

"I'm sorry," he whispered. "I don't know if you can hear me, Dad, but I'm sorrier than I've ever been in my life. I loved you so much. I still do."

One thing he was certain of, he'd make sure everyone in town knew what a stand-up guy his father had been. Hatred for his dad's murderer burned brightly inside him.

He would restore his father's name for both of them. He wasn't sure how yet, but he would find a way.

Not quite ready to go back into the house, he finished unloading the trailer. He wondered what Patience might think.

The thought of her sweet face as she touched his cheek was enough to cause his chest to tighten again. There'd been such honesty in her voice. Her eyes had held tears for him, and for all the pain he'd been through.

As Cade put the last bale on the pile he'd made, he heard a car pulling up on the gravel.

Grabbing a towel from his truck, he wiped his face and hands on it.

"Sheriff."

"Cade, good to see you. Looks like you've been busy."

"We've got a ways to go before we get there, but I am making progress. What brings you out here?"

The sheriff glanced away for a moment. "I have to talk to Patience about something."

"How did you know she was here?"

"She called me. Is she in the house?" The sheriff studied him for a moment.

Cade nodded. "What's going on? Is it about my father's case? Did you find out who killed him?"

The sheriff strode past him toward the porch. "I'm not at liberty to say. Right now what we have is circumstantial, but I think Patience may have found some real evidence. That's why I need to talk to her."

"Then by all means let's go in and have a chat." Cade's tone betrayed his renewed anger.

"It would be best if you stayed out here and let us sort this out. I promise you as soon as we know for certain, either myself or Patience will tell you everything."

What were these people thinking? "No, Sheriff. The secrets stop here. Who killed my father?"

The walkie-talkie on Beau's shoulder squawked, "We've got him, Sheriff."

The sheriff replied quickly. "Put him in the jail and do not let anyone else in there." He gave Cade the once-over. "No visitors, you understand? That includes the mayor and her grandchildren."

"Yes, sir."

Instead of going into the house, the sheriff back-tracked and opened the door to Cade's truck. He pulled the keys out of the ignition and stuck them in his pocket.

"Care to explain?" The words were ground out between clenched teeth. Whatever the sheriff and Patience were up to, Cade had had enough.

"We'd better go inside," Beau said as he climbed onto the porch.

Cade followed him into his father's office.

"Patience." The sheriff held out his hand.

She shook it. "Thanks for coming out here, Beau." She glanced at Cade and frowned.

"Show me what you found," the sheriff said.

Motioning him to come around to the other side of the desk she gave up her seat to him. "This is the kicker," she pointed out. "Everything is time-stamped and dated."

Patience glanced up at Cade, her eyes tight with

worry. Whatever she'd found, it was enough to get someone arrested.

Cade stayed in the doorway. His temper wasn't exactly in check and he had to force himself to think clearly. Why were they keeping the truth from him? They had no right to do it. The victim was his father.

"Well, this gives us motive. It's certainly enough for me to talk to him officially." The sheriff gathered up the documents and folded them against his side. "Once I speak to him, maybe we'll find out if the others were involved. Patience, you can tell him everything after I leave."

"Okay." Her voice was shaky and she glanced at Cade nervously.

The stubborn part of him refused to move aside so Beau could get through the door.

"Cade, let me by. I don't want to have to arrest you for obstructing justice."

"You've got my keys."

"Yep, and I'll send them back with one of the deputies in an hour or so. That should give you time enough to calm down."

"I'm not some idiot who is going to go off all half-cocked. I just want to know who in the hell killed my father."

Beau patted his shoulder. "Understandable that you're frustrated, son."

Cade shifted and allowed Beau to pass.

Cade's attention shifted to Patience who had gone pale. She was ill.

All his anger dissipated.

He immediately guided her to the sofa, but she pulled out of his arms and ran for the door.

PATIENCE MADE IT TO THE EDGE of the driveway before being sick. Her stomach wouldn't stop roiling, and her knees shook with weakness.

A hand pulled back her hair as she doubled over again.

Embarrassed he was there to witness her weakness, she waved him away, but her stomach heaved again.

This time Cade swept her up in his arms and carried her to the truck.

"I'm okay," she said. "Really."

"No, you aren't." He jumped up and sat next to her on the tailgate, handing her a bottle of water. "Sip this." He opened her other hand. "And these are peppermint, they'll help."

After swallowing some of the water, she popped two of the mints in her mouth. Cade sat beside her and rubbed her back.

She took a deep breath. "Bad case of nerves," she said uneasily. "Sorry about that. Not one of my best moments."

"Are you sure it's just nerves?"

She shrugged. "I might have some kind of bug, but I feel better right now. I've been so tied up in knots today and I didn't like keeping things from you, Cade. I really didn't."

He squeezed her closer to him. "I shouldn't have gotten upset. I know you're just doing your job, as is the sheriff. But you can tell me the truth now."

She began by explaining about the gash she found in the tree and her thought that it was made by a rifle. Then she told him the truth about what happened with Harold out by the grave and the records she'd found in his dad's office.

"There were lease agreements in your dad's safe. We know that Harold was involved, but we don't know about the other names on the agreements. A couple of them are the ranchers who have given me a hard time. The water rights around here are a complex web, but from what I can tell, the ranchers wanted to lease land from your dad that had natural-fed wells. He'd drawn up the agreements. What I don't understand is why Harold was arguing with your father. I'm no legal expert, but everything looked straightforward. Maybe they were arguing over the cost? Hopefully, the sheriff will get Harold to confess. It'll make everything much easier if he does."

Cade was completely quiet as he stared off into the horizon.

After sitting for a few minutes more, she slid off the tailgate. Her legs were a little stronger and she had to clean up the office. She'd left the other files out on the desk and the box with Cade's baby things.

Cade grabbed her hand and pulled her to him.

He wrapped his arms around her and held her tight between his legs. "Thank you," he whispered.

She'd given him closure and no one understood how important that was more than she did. Not trusting herself to speak, she squeezed him tight hoping he could feel how much she cared for him.

While the outcome wasn't ideal, he knew what had happened to Joseph. More than anything Patience wanted that kind of closure for herself.

19

BACK AT THE B AND B, Patience sat on the top step of the stairs, listening to Cade relay the events of the day. The sheriff had since wrestled a full confession out of Harold, and he'd been shipped off to Austin for processing.

She hadn't wanted to intrude on the Randalls, but she also wanted to stay close to Cade.

"All these years that man has given me such a hard time about everything," his grandmother said vehemently. "He was the first one to start the rumors in town about your father and he supported my opponents every time I ran for mayor. I thought he just didn't like women. I thought I was a better woman than this, but I hope he suffers like hell."

The other cousins, the ones who lived in Phosphor and those still in town for the festival, were outraged, accident or not. Cade calmed them down.

"Patience and the sheriff have built a strong

case against Harold and with his confession, there's no question he'll get what he deserves," Cade told them.

"That girl deserves a medal," GG said. "Solved a twenty-year-old case in less than a week."

Patience wouldn't want any medal. Honestly she felt as though she'd stumbled through the whole thing. If Harold hadn't made the mistake of driving out to the grave site... Her detective friend, Shannon, had told her half of what they did was sheer dumb luck of being in the right place at the right time. Patience believed her now.

Packing was next on her list. As much as she didn't want to leave town or Cade, she needed to get back to Austin and process the evidence she'd found. Since she was an expert in this area, the sheriff and district attorney agreed that she should do any testing.

Gathering her clothes from the closet, she carefully folded everything and placed it in her suitcase.

The last week had been a wild ride and she remembered again why she enjoyed the calm confines of her lab. But would she be happy going back to that?

Yes. The unfamiliar emotions she'd experienced the last few days had shaken her to her core. Still, she'd survived and solved the case.

Admittedly, leaving Cade would tear her heart out. In some ways he already had.

Her logical side said they'd latched onto one another so intensely because they'd shared the same sort of tragedy. She had lost Jeremy, and Cade, his father. She had been out of sorts with her first time detecting, and he had been recovering from the shock of discovering his father had been murdered. It was no wonder they had reached out to each other for comfort, but that was all it was.

That's why she needed to make the break as quickly as possible. It was the best thing for both of them.

Sighing, she stood and snapped her small suitcase closed. She had to stop by and give Andy and Celia the check for the antiques she'd bought at the festival before she returned to Austin. Downstairs she was almost glad the family had gone their separate ways so she could tell Cade goodbye.

Truthfully, she didn't want to go through all the questions they might have about why she was leaving so abruptly. She had grown to love the Randall family the past few days, but they were a nosey bunch, in the very best sense. Besides, she would have enough to explain once she found Cade.

Never one for small towns, she'd grown to enjoy Phosphor during her short stay. With a few exceptions, the people were friendly and they certainly cared for and looked after one another. It was commendable and not something you found everywhere.

Yes, Phosphor was different from any other place she'd been—and she'd been all over the world.

A quick glance out the window revealed it was dusk and the place was already filled with fireflies.

The tiny insects did look like fairies flying here and there. Instantly she recalled her night under the waterfall with Cade. That had to be one of the most intimate moments of her life, and one she would treasure long after they parted.

She sighed again. She'd never connected to anyone like she had Cade, and she wondered what it would be like to date in Austin, away from the cocoon of Phosphor. Would they have the time? Cade was preoccupied with the follow-up to his company's merger, meanwhile, Stonegate was never short of cases. She could work morning till midnight, but was that the life she wanted?

Maybe she was just scared?

What if their magic simply didn't last? Wouldn't they both be worse off than if they ended it now?

Stop being silly, and grow up. It was a fling, and now it's back to the real world.

"Where are you going?"

Cade stared down at her suitcase.

"I told you. I have to process those samples I took from the site."

Cade frowned.

"It's Saturday night. No one else is working. And the sheriff has his confession."

She shrugged. "Cade, this isn't my only case. I have to get back to my lab. Certainly it won't hurt for the sheriff to have his evidence as soon as possible."

"But you don't have to do it tonight. It's late and you shouldn't be out on country roads in the dark."

She rolled her eyes.

Why can't he understand that it's better if we just get this over with now?

Cade reached for her. "Give me one more night, please. I care for you and I'm not ready for you to go."

She smiled at him. "It's been so good here with you, but it's over. What we had here wasn't real."

Cade bent his head and kissed her, the kind that set fire from her heart to her toes and left her breathless when he stopped.

"Doesn't get any more real than that, Patience. Do you think when we get back to Austin that this is going to be over? I care about you. Let's find out if we could have a future together."

Patience stepped back. "It's all too fast, Cade. I need time and so do you. I'm glad we were both here for one another, but we knew going in this was temporary."

"No, I didn't know that." His eyes narrowed. "Stay tonight and let me show you what we have."

Patience placed a hand against his heart. "We're two people who came together at a difficult time and survived it. Like I said, Cade, what you're feeling isn't real."

"The hell it isn't," Cade said. "I may not have been in a lot of relationships, but I know this is different. Trust me, Patience."

Deep in her soul she wondered if his words were true. "You might be right, but I'm not ready for whatever this is. I don't do this." She waved a hand toward him. "I don't do relationships. Any kind. Someone always gets hurt in the end."

"Patience, you've helped me to see that there's so much more when you can forgive yourself and others. I thought I'd helped you do the same. Are you saying you don't have feelings for me?"

Frustrated, Patience walked away from him. "Of course I do. You're right. What we have is different, but I can't know that for sure unless you give me the time to figure it out. You're pushing so hard, Cade, and as much I want to go with you on whatever ride this is, for my own sanity I have to step back."

Cade faced her. "You can step back as much as you want, I'm not going anywhere."

Patience released a long breath and gathered her thoughts. "I can see why you've been so successful in your business enterprises. Like I said before—"

He held up a hand.

"Yes. Okay. For the record we only met two weeks ago, and I haven't been able to get you out of my mind since. I'm a man who's found the love of his life and he's worried she'll try to slip away."

"You can't love me. That's something that grows as you get to know someone. Maybe lust, Cade, but what you feel isn't love."

He smiled at her. "And you're basing this on your experience with past relationships? Maybe you don't love me, but I most certainly love you."

"That's what's scaring me. I just need—"

Her words were cut off with a kiss, one that seared her soul. Her eyes closed at the initial contact but she opened them to find him watching her as he kissed her. There was so much passion and love in those beautiful eyes of his.

This man loved her.

When he lifted his head, he smiled. "You almost said you needed me."

"You make me feel so— I don't know what I'm saying."

"That's it. I make you *feel*. You've spent so long closing yourself off to everyone around you that you've forgotten what it's like to feel. You're right. Love is something that grows. I—"

"Cade—"

He put his fingers to her lips. "For now, it's the last night of the festival, come and play with me. I dare you. Give me this one night, and then I'll give you the space you think you need." He kissed her again and this time when their bodies touched she knew she had lost the argument.

"Fine," she whispered against his lips. "But I leave first thing tomorrow morning."

"Got it." He smiled.

"With one condition."

He leaned back from her. "What?"

She tugged him toward the stairs.

"Oh." He followed her. "That's one condition I don't mind at all."

20

CADE PLACED HIS ARM ON HER shoulders and pulled Patience close as they reached the top of the Ferris wheel. After making love, they'd finally made it to the midway.

So far he'd won her a stuffed bear that looked like it had seen better days and an expandable ring with a giant plastic pink diamond on it. The delight in her eyes when he handed her the cheesy prizes was something that made his heart do double-time.

"This is so much fun." She stuck her right hand out to show off her fake ring. "I can't remember the last time I've been on a Ferris wheel. I had to be ten, at the most."

"It's been a while for me, too." Cade kissed the top of her head. He struggled to believe she wanted to make a clean break.

Cade was worried, he'd never felt like this about a woman. He knew she was skittish and that commitment wasn't something that came easy for her. Hell, attachments period were difficult for her.

He was also certain that had a great deal to do with her brother's disappearance. She was afraid to care too much for someone. That was something he understood. Finding out the truth about his father had changed his life, and he wished he could return the favor. More than once this evening he'd thought about hiring the SIA to find out what had happened to her brother, but he knew her well enough to understand she'd feel betrayed if he went behind her back. The issue with her brother was something she had to come to terms with on her own.

They made another revolution to the top of the Ferris wheel. He wondered if this was the right time, but decided to hell with it. Reaching into his pocket, he pulled out the fairy necklace he'd bought for her the other night. "I want to give you something, so you'll remember our time together," he whispered.

She tilted her face up toward him. "Cade, I have my bear and my fancy ring, and trust me I'm never going to forget."

He held out the necklace. "I won't forget, either, but I saw this and it reminded me of you." He pushed up her hair and placed it around her neck.

She picked up the tiny fairy and smiled. "It's beautiful. I love it. But you didn't have to do this."

"I want you to take a little piece of Phosphor and me home with you."

She kissed him then, to a chorus of wolf whistles and "Get a room," from the fairgoers below.

Her phone rang interrupting their bliss.

She checked the number, and then put the phone to her ear. "Mar, what's up. Yep, I sent you the report. Oh, my phone doesn't have the best service here. I didn't see his calls on my voice mail. What? When?" Patience glanced at her watch. "I need two hours to get to my apartment and then another hour to pack and get to the airport. Where was it in Italy? Ah, yes. I know it well. I didn't realize that's where he was. Yeah, I'll meet you at the airport."

They'd reached the bottom of the ride and the door swung open so they could get out. "Cade, I've got to go now. I'm sorry."

"Go where, Italy?"

She nodded. "I can't tell you the details, though believe me I want to, but the case involves my dad and a dig he's working on. I've got to get there as fast as possible."

She was leaving him, but she needed help, and he had a way to do that.

"Call your friend back and tell her to cancel the flights. Let her know you'll meet her at hangar eleven."

"Cade, I don't have time—"

"I'm sending you on my private jet. It's not the company's. It's mine. My pilot is always on standby."

They'd left the fairgrounds and reached his truck. He helped her in.

"That's too much. I can't let you do this."

"Patience, you just solved my father's murder. Helped me know how much he loved me. There's no price on that. Besides, if you take commercial flights, that's going to cost you more time. My plane stops for twenty minutes in Atlanta, and you'll be on your way."

"Cade, this is crazy."

"Patience, call your friend. Better yet, dial the number and give me the phone. I'll do that while you finish packing. Then I'll take you to the airport."

They arrived at the B and B.

"I have my car. I can't just leave it here."

"I'll have Logan drive it back to Austin. We drove down together. So it's no big deal." He held up a hand. "Please, let me take care of you. You've been taking care of me the past few days. I want to do these things for you."

She stared at him for a moment then reached into her purse. "I hope Logan will fit in my SUV." She handed him the keys.

Cade jumped out and opened her door. He followed her upstairs and threw his stuff in a bag, too. He'd check in at work on Monday, make sure everything was going okay, before he came back to Phosphor.

"He's a friend. Uh, yes, that kind of friend," Patience told her colleague, using her cell again.

Cade bet her colleague would have all kinds of questions once they boarded the plane.

They were at Patience's condo in an hour and a half, and while she repacked he checked out her place. It was stark and everything was the same neutral color from the walls, to the furniture and floors. But she did have some art on the wall, which spoke volumes about the woman he'd come to love.

There were playful folk art paintings next to modern masters.

"I'm ready." She came out of the bedroom in a gray striped suit with her beautiful hair in a tight bun. Still, she was the most beautiful woman he'd ever seen.

"Oh, wait." She pulled out the case where she carried the evidence bags. Picking up her phone, she dialed a number.

"Scott, yeah, sorry to call so late. Listen, I'm sending you a priority. It's evidence for a case and I want it handled the way I would do it. Do you understand me?" Her voice had a slight edge. This was the straightforward woman he'd met that first day. "The courier will have it to you in the morning and I'll email specifics tonight. Got it?"

Thirty minutes later, they pulled up to the hangar. Her colleague was already there with a man.

Patience introduced them as Mar and Jackson. They were married and Mar owned Stonegate. There was something in Jackson's eyes that told Cade the man had seen more than any person should, but he was glad he'd be there to protect Patience.

"We'll pay you back for the cost of the plane," Mar promised.

"No, you won't." His arm slid around Patience's waist. "I'm doing this for her."

"Uh, I think we should probably board," Jackson ushered his wife to the plane.

"You really are amazing." Patience hugged Cade hard.

He bent down to kiss her and his gut tightened with the knowledge that this would be the last time he saw her for a while. Part of him wanted to follow her on the plane, but he knew that wasn't possible. She needed time and he had his own business to look after.

"I'll call you. I don't really know specifics. I have no idea how long I'll be gone." She hugged his neck and then pulled away. "I've got to go."

"Patience?"

She stopped on the first step of the stairs leading up to the plane. "Yeah?"

"I'll be here when you get back."

He enjoyed the small smile on her lips.

ON THE PLANE, PATIENCE, MAR and Jackson video conferenced with her father about what he'd found on his dig. Several human skeletons had been discovered and he believed they dated back several hundred years. But he had to prove that to the police right away or his dig would become a crime scene. That's where Mar and Jackson came in. Stonegate had helped the authorities catch a murderer a few months ago and Mar was going to use her contacts to give Patience enough time to examine the bones and date them. Jackson was there for security purposes. The former CIA agent also knew people in Italy and would help to protect the site. Her father had looked older than she remembered. Though his cheeks had been pink with excitement while he was talking about his dig.

Mar turned back in her seat. "He let you borrow his private jet?"

Patience opened her eyes to see Mar giving her a curious look.

"He's a nice guy." Patience smiled at her friend.

"I know a lot of nice guys, but they don't loan me their private planes."

"I would—if I had one," Jackson chimed in. His eyes were closed as he reclined in his seat, but he had a silly grin on his face.

Mar kissed his cheek. "Babe, that's why I love you."

She turned back to Patience, who was seated on the sofa across from their two chairs.

The jet was decorated better than her apartment and had every amenity one could imagine, including a full bath and a large galley-style kitchen with a chef, who had informed them that he'd made snacks and would have breakfast ready by six the next morning.

"So, he must be really happy about you solving his

father's murder." Mar wasn't going to give up until Patience told her the truth.

"Yes, he was grateful. Like I said, he's a great guy."

Mar's eyebrow went up.

Patience rolled her eyes for the second time that night. "We bonded. What do you want me to say?"

Mar giggled. "Bonded? Wow. I've never heard it called that. It's obvious he's pretty into you. I could tell that from just the way he looked at you."

Patience had seen that look, too, and it had been all she could do not to beg him to jump on the plane with her. Unfortunately, she'd seen what a distraction he could be and she hadn't lied about needing space.

The trip had come at an excellent time. The time apart would give them the opportunity to cool off a bit and see how they really feel. Though, her feelings wouldn't change. She loved the guy. Oh, she'd given him a line about not really knowing, but she did.

"So, it's that intense?" Mar gave her a curious look.

"Yes." Patience had been staring off into space so turned her attention back to her friend. "But you know me. I don't normally do strong emotional attachments, and I need time to sort this out."

"Patience, there's no sorting to be done. It's written all over your face. You're in love with him."

"That may be true, but I'm not ready. You know I wasn't looking for anything right now. My life is so full. I don't know that I would have time for a relationship, not the kind he would want."

Mar harrumphed. "If he's worth it, then you make the time. That's how it works. You're right. Your life is full—of work. But take it from me—work isn't everything. You'll wake up some day incredibly lonely and wondering why you chose your career over love."

"Mar—"

"There's nothing wrong with loving your job, as long as you have someone to share it with. If you care about this guy, you have to find a way to make it work."

"Well, I guess if you can do it, anyone can." Patience winked at her.

Jackson guffawed and Mar chuckled.

"I'm not sure I've ever heard you make a joke like that," Mar said. "I like what he's doing for you already."

"Are you saying I'm uptight?" Patience asked even though she knew the answer.

Jackson grunted.

"Maybe more cautious than most people I know," Mar answered. "I think this is the longest conversation we've ever had and I consider you one of my dearest friends. You've never been one to express yourself."

Her friend was right. "There was something about his family, and, well, him. I'm more relaxed than I've ever been when I was around them. They give each other a hard time, but they're all so close, kind of like we are at the agency. They would do anything for one another. I guess you're right. He did help me see things from a different perspective."

Cade had opened a new world to her, one, if she were completely honest with herself, she was more than anxious to explore.

21

As THE JET LANDED ON THE tarmac, Patience smiled. She was finally home. When the door opened she expected to see Cade, but there was a driver there instead.

"Dr. Clark?"

She nodded.

"Mr. Randall asked that I take you wherever you need to go. He's been caught up in a meeting and says he regrets not being able to meet you."

She didn't bother to hide her disappointment, but she understood. Every day for three weeks Cade had called Patience. Most of the time they didn't have long to talk, but they both enjoyed staying connected. Without giving specifics about the project she was working on with her dad, she'd been able to bounce ideas off him. He, in turn, had done the same with her.

While he never said how much, Cade had made

billions in the merger and he poured the majority of it back into the organization. His company was in the middle of building a huge manufacturing plant outside of Austin. It would bring thousands of jobs to the area, and she was proud of him for that.

"Doctor?"

The chauffer held the door for her, and then loaded her case in the back of the car. Thanks to Cade she'd been able to sleep most of the way there. He'd insisted she take his jet back, and except for the flight attendant and pilots, she'd been the only passenger. Mar and Jackson had flown to London to check on Stonegate's new office there.

After weeks of only getting a few hours of sleep a night, it had been heaven to stretch out on one of the jet's comfy couches. In fact, she felt like a new woman.

"Can you drop me at my condo?" She gave him the address, and it wasn't long before they were in front of her building.

The driver insisted on carrying her case upstairs, even though it rolled and there was an elevator. After he left, she took a quick shower and put on a pair of jeans and T-shirt to go to the office. It was Friday afternoon, but she wanted to file her reports and check with her assistants at the lab to make sure everything was up-to-date.

As she was getting ready to leave, she felt another stabbing pain in her gut. She doubled over for a moment and tried to remember the last time she ate.

She probably needed something in her stomach and to take her meds.

In Italy her father had taken her stomach pains seriously and insisted on accompanying her to the emergency room. They had run a variety of tests. The doctors discovered she had an ulcer, one that could be treated with antibiotics.

They had warned her to stay away from the marinara sauce and to reduce her stress. While she'd been careful with the food, there was no way she could keep herself from being nervous, especially when she would soon see Cade. They had talked the night before and he'd been excited about seeing her. But when he didn't show up as promised to meet her, well, the doubts sunk in.

When her stomach settled she grabbed her keys and headed to the office. If there was one thing that could keep her from obsessing about what might be happening with Cade, it was her work.

"Hey, boss, you're back. We didn't expect you in until Monday," one of her assistants greeted her.

"You know me, Chris, had to check in." She plopped her keys on the steel table.

He laughed. "You wouldn't be you if you didn't. Scott is in the photo lab developing some of the pictures you guys sent back from Rome. I can't believe your dad uncovered eleven-hundred-year-old bones. What a find."

"Yeah. He was pretty excited, and he'll have all

the time in the world he needs to complete the dig now that they've registered it as a historic site."

Working with her father, she had been the one to identify the age of the bones, which had been verified by several leading scientists in Rome.

One of the best things about her trip was she and her father had several very frank conversations about everything that was going on in their lives. In many ways it was like they were before Jeremy had disappeared. Though it had been difficult, they'd even discussed that they would once again hire professionals to search for Jeremy. It was a burden they no longer carried alone, as her stepmother, Jenny, was also adamant in being involved.

Jenny and the boys were in Italy with her father, and for the first time Patience had genuinely connected with them in a way that made her feel like a part of the family. Her twin stepbrothers, who were eleven, were fascinated by her work and became fairly good assistants once they learned that science sometimes takes time.

Even though she spent eighteen hours a day working, she still managed to spend time with her family.

"Any chance we'll get to see those bones?" Chris interrupted her thoughts.

She shook her head. "I'm afraid they're now owned by the Italian government since it was on their property. Though they did ask me to come back to see if I can't help identify who they belong to."

"And you'll take us, right?" He waggled his eyebrows.

Patience understood the excitement over a find like this. "I'll take it under consideration."

"Hey, boss, here are your up close and personals," Scott said as he closed the photo lab door. "I noticed two of the femurs were an odd size, did you guys figure out why?"

"Dwarfism," she said. "But that's one of the reasons I took so many photos. I have a feeling this could be a long-term project for us."

She glanced at her watch. "Why don't you guys clean up and get out of here. You've been working double duty for me and the London office for the last three weeks. You deserve some time off."

Chris and Scott gave each other a strange look.

"What?" Patience held up her hands in a questioning motion.

"You—well, you seem different." Chris fidgeted. "You're usually so intense."

Patience smiled. "I'm still intense, guys, but this is my one day out of three hundred and sixty-five that I'm feeling generous. Take advantage of it. Because Monday I'm back to making your lives a living hell." She gave them a wink and went back to her paperwork.

"You don't have to tell us twice," Scott said.

They both locked their research away and stored the equipment they'd been using.

Patience laughed as they all but ran out the door.

CADE WATCHED PATIENCE FOR several minutes from the door of her lab. She was as beautiful as the last time he'd seen her, maybe even more so. Whatever she was thinking, she had a serious look on her face and she chewed on her lip as if she were nervous. She also fingered the necklace he'd given her, which she promised she hadn't taken off since the night he'd given it to her.

"Did you miss me?"

Patience jumped and nearly fell off the stool she'd been sitting on.

"You surprised me." Her hand flew against her chest as she moved to greet him. "And yes—" she wrapped her arms around his neck "—I missed you."

When their lips met, Cade's body went rigid with need. He'd more than missed her. This woman held his heart so tightly and he didn't think she had a clue.

He'd spent the last two weeks trying to figure out how he could get her to marry him as fast as possible. Never in his life had he wanted or needed someone like he did Patience.

"From the, um, feel of things it seems you must have missed me, too." She pressed herself tight against his already hardening erection.

"Oh, you don't know the half of it. Every time we talked on the phone, well, let's just say it's been a long few weeks."

They kissed.

"Are you in the middle of something?" He pointed to her computer and quipped, "Because I'd really like to take you home and ravish you."

"Mmm. Ravishing does sound good." She cleared her desk and shut off her laptop.

The lab was orderly, just the way she liked it, he was certain. It still boggled his mind that she was so prim and proper and at the same time one of the most sensual creatures he'd ever met in his life.

22

CADE'S HOME WAS NOTHING short of magnificent. The modern glass-and-steel structure jutted out over Lake Travis with incredible hillside views. One side of the house was nothing but windows. Patience kept forgetting how wealthy Cade was. He was so down-to-earth and in Phosphor his life was much more simple.

They were outside on the deck where Cade had grilled their steaks. After weeks of the bland pasta the doctors had insisted on and soups, the steak tasted heavenly. What made it so special was that Cade had consulted with his cousin Kent, who was a doctor, about the types of foods she could eat.

"Patience." Cade suddenly looked nervous. "I have something I need to talk to you about."

She crossed her legs in the chair and leaned forward. "Whatever it is, you're scaring me." She couldn't imagine what he could be thinking. "Are you sick? Did something happen to GG?"

He laughed and his tone made her feel a little better.

"This isn't the romantic way I'd planned this, but—I want to warn you that I'm going to ask you an important question."

Patience was still clueless.

"I want to ask you to marry me."

He could have said he had ten giraffes in the backyard and she wouldn't have been any more surprised. They'd only known each other a short time, and though she'd fantasized about marriage more than once this was much faster than she expected.

Cade held up his hand. "I'm not expecting an answer right away. I just want you to get used to the idea." He pulled out a box and opened it. A huge emerald cut diamond glittered in the porch light. "But when you feel like you are ready to wear this, you say the word. I love you, Patience. I love you more than anyone or anything in this world."

"I—this is…" She couldn't quite get the words out. Part of her wanted to grab the ring, and the other part wanted to order him to take her home. "It's sudden," she finally said.

They sat in silence for a few moments and she tried to digest everything he'd said. He loved her. But marriage?

Cade shook his head. "This was too soon. I knew better. Please, forget I did this. We can wait. I just wanted you to see—" He started to rise, but she grabbed his hands.

"I love you, too," she said softly, tears brimming in her eyes.

He stopped as if he hadn't heard her correctly.

"I mean it, Cade, I've loved you pretty much ever since I met you."

"That's a good start." He leaned down and kissed her hands. "Honestly, I wanted to give you time to get used to the idea before I really popped the question."

She laughed nervously still trying to decide how she felt about the idea of Cade wanting to marry her. "If you want to go steady first, you don't need a ring that big. In fact, I think you're supposed to give me your class ring on a chain or something."

He sat back down and smiled at her.

"I'm the kind of person who always thinks big," he said as he pulled her into his lap. "Please don't be upset. Part of me was worried some Italian Romeo would sweep you off your feet and the idea was nothing short of torture for me." He squeezed his arms around her.

"The only Romeo I'm interested in is you. For the record, I'm not saying no. Just not a yes right this second. And by the way, you picked out the most gorgeous ring I've ever seen. Will you keep it safe for me?"

"Yes," he said as he nuzzled her neck sending shivers down her spine.

"Cade," she whispered as he trailed kisses down her back.

"Uh-huh?"

"Let me show you how much I love you."

Scooping her up, Cade carried her to the bedroom.

AFTER A NIGHT OF LOVEMAKING, Cade needed to satisfy another primal instinct, so he headed down to the kitchen.

You almost blew everything.

Hell, don't I know it.

The ring had been too much for her. The shock in her eyes alone had created a knot of fear in his gut.

What the hell were you thinking?

That I love her.

He hadn't lied about the Italian Romeo. She was so beautiful and had such a kind heart. Men were drawn to her and she didn't have a clue. He'd seen it time and time again when they were in Phosphor. He couldn't get over that she was his woman.

His woman. She'd laugh if she heard him say that out loud, but it was true. She was it for him.

The idea of spending another day without waking up next to her was hard to imagine. She brought a kind of balance to his life that he never realized he needed.

He only hoped he did the same for her. When she'd shared with Cade her discussions with her dad, even via the phone he could tell how much mending that relationship had lightened her soul. She'd told him that it was after seeing him with GG and his cousins that she realized how much she was missing out on with her own family.

He'd also been impressed by the way she was able to wrap her quick mind around the details of his business and she had fresh perspective, which was exactly what he needed.

That connection they'd forged in Phosphor had only grown stronger as the days went on. When he found out they'd taken her to the emergency room he'd made preparations to fly to Italy. But she'd called him an hour later to tell him that she was fine.

"Is that bacon?" Patience covered her mouth in a yawn as she sauntered into the kitchen wearing his shirt from the night before. Her long, toned legs and her tousled hair took his breath away.

"I'm not sure the bacon is good for your ulcer, but I'm also making eggs," he said as he gathered her in his arms and kissed her.

She tugged on his ear. "I don't care if it's good for me or not, I'm eating bacon. Maybe I'll even have seconds."

The feel of her against him was too much for his control. Gently he set her on the kitchen counter. "I have a better idea of what I want for breakfast," he said, cupping her left breast.

Her breath hitched as he rubbed his thumb across her nipple. Unbuttoning the shirt he used his tongue on one breast, then the other. Her hands went to his hair as she gasped.

The sound caused a tent in his boxers.

When her hand reached down into said boxers, he nearly came in her hand.

His fingers flew down to her heat and when he discovered she didn't have on panties, he stopped breathing for a moment. He captured her lips with his as he slid his fingers into her pink flesh.

Patience moaned and writhed against him.

Increasing the speed of his fingers he teased her flesh faster and harder until she screamed her release.

She shuddered and leaned into him, head bent. "I want you, Cade. Please, I need you inside me," she begged.

More than anything he wanted to, but they were missing a key element.

"Patience, I don't have a condom."

She gave him a wicked smile as she pulled one out of the breast pocket of the shirt she was wearing.

That's when he saw it. She wore the engagement ring.

Everything stopped as he stared at her hand.

She laughed at the shock he knew was on his face.

"Patience, did you come down here to seduce me into marrying you?"

"Yes," she whispered as she opened the condom. "I dare you to marry me, Cade Randall."

"Oh, hell, yeah," he said as her fingers slid the condom down his cock. "I'll take that dare any day, but are you sure?"

"Oh, yeah," she said as she guided him into her. The tightness and warmth was almost his undoing. Then she kissed him and Cade's body took over as he pumped in and out of her slowly.

"Tell me how much you love me, baby," he said.

She watched him with those knowing eyes of hers. "With everything that I am. Do you want to marry me, Cade Randall?" she asked, as she leaned back on the counter making it easier for him to get his full length into her.

"Yes," he growled. "I want you more than anything I've ever wanted in my life."

"Then take me, Cade, take me."

Epilogue

Nine months later

"CADE, WE'RE FIFTEEN MINUTES out. Are Patience and her dad there?" Patience's boss Mariska had called to check in with him.

"They're upstairs unpacking, they'll be down here in a few minutes," he answered. "Is everything all right?"

"Definitely," Mar affirmed. "Hold on, Jackson wants to talk to you."

"Hey, man, I know Mar sounds nervous, but it's all good. The package is ready." Jackson was not just Mariska's husband, but a former CIA agent. They were coming to Phosphor for the wedding and now they had what he hoped would be the best present ever for Patience.

Cade took a deep breath. There was a noise at the top of the stairs. "Thanks for this," he whispered into the phone. "Just text me when you guys are coming up the walk. I don't know if I should give them some kind of warning or let it be a surprise."

"A package this big should be a surprise," Jackson said.

Cade couldn't argue that, and besides, he had no idea how he could explain what was about to happen. Never in his life had he been this nervous. All he wanted was for Patience to be happy.

Patience talked him into holding off on the wedding until her dad could come back to the States from Italy. Normally a control freak with a capital *F* she'd left most of the planning to GG, who had done her level best to involve the entire town. There were banners congratulating the couple and twinkle lights on every tree.

Smiling, he watched Patience chat with her father, Professor Clark, as they entered the living room. Thanks to her work on his archeological dig, they had spent more time together in the past few months than they had since she went away to college. Every day he saw those walls she kept erected around herself crumble more and more.

His phone vibrated. This was it.

"Everything okay?" Cade asked.

"Fine," Patience's father answered.

That was good. They would need some calm before the storm.

The door creaked open and Mar stepped through.

"Mar!" Patience rushed up to give the woman a hug. "I didn't know you were coming down today."

GG stepped up beside Cade. He gave her a worried glance and she put a hand on his shoulder. She, along with Patience's stepmother, were the only two people at the B and B who knew what was about to happen.

"It'll be all right, son," she tried to reassure him.

As she said the words, Patience's brother, Jeremy, stepped through the door. He was a tall, gangly fellow, with the same curly blond hair as his sister's, though, his was cut short.

There was a loud gasp. "Jeremy?" The professor reached out a hand to the boy.

Patience had been hugging Mar and was faced away from the young man, but she quickly whipped around at the sound of his name.

A sob came from her throat and she, too, reached out to Jeremy. He looked from one to the other as if he wasn't sure what he should do.

Patience swallowed hard and then smiled. "Is it really you?"

The young man nodded.

"Do you know who we are?" Her voice was no more than a whisper.

"Yes." Jeremy's wobbly voice was hoarse.

Her father stood there with tears streaming down his face. "Son?" He extended his arms full out and this time Jeremy did the same, hugging his father as they sobbed in each other's arms. Patience wrapped her arms around them both.

Cade glanced around the room and there wasn't a

dry eye anywhere. GG, who rarely cried, dabbed her eyes with a kitchen towel. Then she motioned Mar, Jackson and him to join her in the kitchen.

"Let's give them some. time alone," she said softly.

As they were turning to go, Cade noticed Patience's stepmother at the top of the stairs. She held a box of tissues. He motioned for her to come down, but she mouthed, "Have to look after the boys." He nodded his understanding.

With one more glance back at Patience and her family, he smiled.

"How could someone steal a child?" Patience asked Cade as they snuggled on the couch in the family room at the B and B. The fire was roaring and the smell of fresh pine boughs twisted over the mantel filled the air.

It had been nearly six hours since her brother walked through the door and she still couldn't wrap her mind around it.

"There's no excuse for what your aunt did," Cade answered, "but at least Jeremy grew up loved. And he's a good guy, that's easy to see. Your mother's sister might have been crazy, but she took proper care of him."

Patience kissed Cade's cheek. "He is a great guy. I'm not surprised he's an artist. He used to draw on everything." She sighed happily. "We're all together, Cade. You brought us all together for our wedding."

He wrapped one of her curls around his finger. "You can thank your friends Shannon, Mar and Jackson and the rest of the Stonegate gang for their truly heroic efforts. They've been working around the clock to find him for you. It was when GG asked if any of your mother's family might want to come that I started digging."

Patience and her father didn't know about her mother's sister. When her mother had married her dad, no one from her side was in attendance. She told him they were all dead. Now that her aunt, Lucille, was dead there was a good chance they would never know the whole story. The woman told Jeremy that Patience and their father had been in a terrible accident and that she had been given custody of him. He was so young then, that he never thought to question her.

"I guess when I was old enough to ask questions I never thought to," Jeremy had said. "We had a happy life and it never dawned on me, until your friend Mar arrived at my college dorm, that she might have lied."

Patience blew out a big breath. "I can't believe this day. Nothing feels real anymore."

Cade took both of her hands in his. "This is real," he said as he kissed her.

She touched his cheek. "In case I've forgotten to say it today, I love you. More than I ever thought it possible to love someone." Leaning away she gave him a wink. "In fact, I'm thinking we should get married or something."

Cade laughed. "Well, we're definitely getting married in forty-eight hours, even if I have to hog-tie you and throw you over my shoulder to get you down the aisle."

She scooted farther away from him. "I only made you wait a few extra months."

"The longest nine months of my life. I've been worried that you were never going to make an honest man out of me."

Patience giggled. He always did know how to make her laugh. It was one of the many qualities that made him such a wonder.

"Cade?"

"Mmm?" He snuggled into her neck.

"I'm so restless. I think I need a good soak in a hot tub."

"Do you want me to go up and get the bath started?"

She stood and grabbed his hand pulling him off the couch. "I was thinking some place a little more private. A magical place where the fairies play."

His eyes lit with understanding. "It's forty degrees outside, hon." But he followed her to the coatrack.

"Yes, but the water will be warm and I feel the need to, um, express myself."

Cade laughed again. "Well, then we better find someplace private."

She opened the door, but before she could walk through he grabbed her and kissed her hard. "I love you, Patience."

Her heart whole for the first time in her life, she took his face between her mitten-covered hands. "Cade. That's what makes my life so amazing." On his lips, she whispered, "I love you, too, Cade. Always."

* * * * *

COMING NEXT MONTH

Available May 31, 2011

#615 REAL MEN WEAR PLAID!
Encounters
Rhonda Nelson

#616 TERMS OF SURRENDER
Uniformly Hot!
Leslie Kelly

#617 RECKLESS PLEASURES
The Pleasure Seekers
Tori Carrington

#618 SHOULD'VE BEEN A COWBOY
Sons of Chance
Vicki Lewis Thompson

#619 HOT TO THE TOUCH
Checking E-Males
Isabel Sharpe

#620 MINE UNTIL MORNING
24 Hours: Blackout
Samantha Hunter

> You can find more information on upcoming
> Harlequin® titles, free excerpts and more at
> **www.HarlequinInsideRomance.com.**

HBCNM0511

REQUEST YOUR FREE BOOKS!
2 FREE NOVELS PLUS 2 FREE GIFTS!

red-hot reads!

Harlequin® Blaze™ brings you
New York Times *and* USA TODAY *bestselling author*
Vicki Lewis Thompson with three new steamy titles
from the bestselling miniseries SONS OF CHANCE

Chance isn't just the last name of these rugged
Wyoming cowboys—it's their motto, too!

Read on for a sneak peek at the first title,
SHOULD'VE BEEN A COWBOY

Available June 2011 only from Harlequin® Blaze™.

"THANKS FOR NOT TURNING ON THE LIGHTS," Tyler said. "I'm a mess."

"Not in my book." Even in low light, Alex had a good view of her yellow shirt plastered to her body. It was all he could do not to reach for her, mud and all. But the next move needed to be hers, not his.

She slicked her wet hair back and squeezed some water out of the ends as she glanced upward. "I like the sound of the rain on a tin roof."

"Me, too."

She met his gaze briefly and looked away. "Where's the sink?"

"At the far end, beyond the last stall."

Tyler's running shoes squished as she walked down the aisle between the rows of stalls. She glanced sideways at Alex. "So how much of a cowboy are you these days? Do you ride the range and stuff?"

"I ride." He liked being able to say that. "Why?"

"Just wondered. Last summer, you were still a city boy. You even told me you weren't the cowboy type, but you're...different now."

He wasn't sure if that was a good thing or a bad thing. Maybe she preferred city boys to cowboys. "How am I different?"

"Well, you dress differently, and your hair's a little longer. Your face seems a little more chiseled, but maybe that's because of your hair. Also, there's something else, something harder to define, an attitude…"

"Are you saying I have an attitude?"

"Not in a bad way. It's more like a quiet confidence."

He was flattered, but still he had to laugh. "I just admitted a while ago that I have all kinds of doubts about this event tomorrow. That doesn't seem like quiet confidence to me."

"This isn't about your job, it's about…your…" She took a deep breath. "It's about your sex appeal, okay? I have no business talking about it, because it will only make me want to do things I shouldn't do." She started toward the end of the barn. "Now, where's that sink? We need to get cleaned up and go back to the house. Dinner is probably ready, and I—"

He spun her around and pulled her into his arms, mud and all. "Let's do those things." Then he kissed her, knowing that she would kiss him back, knowing that this time he would take that kiss where he wanted it to go. And she would let him.

Follow Tyler and Alex's wild adventures in
SHOULD'VE BEEN A COWBOY
Available June 2011 only from Harlequin® Blaze™
wherever books are sold.

Do you need a cowboy fix?

NEW YORK TIMES BESTSELLING AUTHOR
Vicki Lewis Thompson
RETURNS WITH HER SIZZLING TRILOGY...

Sons of Chance

Chance isn't just the last name of these rugged
Wyoming cowboys—it's their motto, too!

Take a chance...on a Chance!

Saddle up with:
SHOULD'VE BEEN A COWBOY (June)
COWBOY UP (July)
COWBOYS LIKE US (August)

**Available from Harlequin® Blaze™
wherever books are sold.**

www.eHarlequin.com

HB79622

HARLEQUIN® HISTORICAL:
Where love is timeless

USA TODAY BESTSELLING AUTHOR

CAROLYN DAVIDSON

INTRODUCES HER
WILD WESTERN HISTORICAL

Saving Grace

SHE IS FIGHTING FOR HER LIFE...
BUT THEIR LOVE CAN HEAL ANYTHING

If ever Grace Benson needs a man to ride to her rescue,
now is the time—and Simon Grafton is the man! When he
encounters her being brutally attacked on the roadside by her
uncle's farmhand, Simon doesn't flinch. He'll risk anything to
defend this innocent from a madman still on the loose.

As Simon helps her heal and gain a new foothold in life,
it becomes clear that his heart is what needs defending.
Soon, his only course of action is to make her his bride....

**Available from Harlequin® Historical
June 2011**